Val's eyes open  She seemed to suck Christina in toward Christina. tina's dangling hair a harvest. "Then Shevvingtons might voice. As if the Shevvingtons' ears were pressed to cracks.

"I live with them," said Christina. "I have to board at Schooner Inne. *Like Anya.*"

"They'll get you," said Val. Suddenly her voice was normal. As if having the Shevvingtons win were also normal.

Christina shook her head. "No, they won't. I know their plan."

"It doesn't help to know their plan. They get the other adults on their side. They get your parents and your teachers. They get psychiatrists. They make up lies. They corner you. They crowd you."

Val's huge eyes stared into a white corner of her white room, as if seeing a white rat there, trapped, caught, destroyed.

"If you're next, and you know it," whispered Val, "you must run." She lay back on her bed. Suddenly she was limp as a wet dishrag. Just clothes lying on the bedcovers, with no body inside them.

"Come back!" said Christina authoritatively.

But Val did not come back.

Books in Caroline B. Cooney's
Point horror trilogy:

Book #1 *The Fog*

Book #2 *The Snow*

Book #3 *The Fire*

620L

THE FIRE

Caroline B. Cooney

SCHOLASTIC INC.
New York Toronto London Auckland Sydney

ISBN 0-590-41641-3

12 11 10 9 8 7   3 4 5/9

Printed in the U.S.A.   01

First Scholastic printing, June 1990

Prologue

At five-thirty in the morning, the rising sun touched the coast of Maine, passed through a window high in Schooner Inne, and rested on a pillow. Strange hair lay on the pillow: silver and gold laced with chocolate brown.

The hair seemed to burn in the sunlight, its three colors melting as if on fire.

In the doorway of the bedroom, someone smiled at the sleeping girl. The smile exposed stubby yellow teeth in a face as flat as paper. Above the smile, eyes glowed like phosphorescent mold. Fingers, whose bitten nails were painted blood-red, lit a match. The match rasped across the striking surface like a knife being sharpened. The yellow smile curled across a complexion like pie dough, and the visitor slid away, down creaking stairs, behind thick green doors.

Chapter 1

Christina Romney woke with a jolt so intense she wondered if thirteen-year-olds ever had heart attacks. She pressed her two hands over her heart to stop it from beating so hard. What woke me? she thought. Christina preferred to take an hour to wake up, slowly sifting away the sleep.

Outside on the ocean, lobster boats roared. One was playing a radio station Christina particularly liked. She hummed along.

She ran her fingers through her hair, taming it. Sometimes she could feel the separate colors, as if the silver and gold and brown grew from different parts of her soul.

She hopped out of bed, dressing quickly. Even in May it was cold in the third-floor bedroom of the old sea captain's house perched on an ocean cliff. Christina needed a long-sleeved shirt, a cotton sweater, and a hooded sweatshirt. One by one, as the day warmed, she would peel them off.

She decided to go down to the wharf and talk to

the lobstermen. She knew most of them. Christina was not from the mainland; she was boarding at Schooner Inne for the school year; her home was Burning Fog Isle, far out at sea.

Eighteen days until summer vacation! Christina exulted. I can last for eighteen days of anything. Even seventh grade. Then I get to go *home*.

She was much, much older than she had been the September before. She wondered if the islanders would see how changed she was. Probably not. She had learned that people saw only your outside. Christina was the only seventh-grader who had not gotten any taller. Perhaps fear was damaging to your height.

She tugged her sweatshirt down over her small flat chest and turned to leave the little attic bedroom.

A long, thin, pale candle was burning by the door. It was stuck in an empty coffee can, leaning sideways, hot wax dripping right onto the floor. The flame leaned toward Christina.

Her heart jolted again and thrashed in her chest like an animal trying to escape. Only a few nights before, she had been sleepwalking. Or so the Shevvingtons claimed. She had ignored them. Christina was solid as granite; she would never do anything as fanciful as sleepwalk.

She bent to look at the candle, and its golden flame leaned toward her, as if to kiss her lips. As if she and the tiny fire were old, intimate friends.

She had a vision of herself staring blankly, creeping silently down all the curving stairs of the mansion, like a blind butterfly, breaking her wings against the walls until she reached the kitchen. Finding a tin can. Finding a candle. Dropping it into the can like a blueberry into a pail and lighting it. Drifting up to the attic again like a ghost, leaving a trail of wax.

Schooner Inne, its timbers centuries old, would burn as easily as crushed newspaper. She would never have brought a burning candle up here.

The candle winked at her. It knew the truth.

She blew it out, but the candle re-lit itself.

She could not wrench her eyes away from the flame. It was shaped like a weeping tear. She knelt beside it, her hair falling forward, like tinder ready to catch fire itself. Holding her hair up in a ponytail, she blew the flame out forcefully. The candle sagged down into the coffee can.

Christina picked it up. Making no noise, she tiptoed out of her room, around the tilting balcony, and down the bare wooden stairs. On the second floor Mr. and Mrs. Shevvington slept. It would not do to awaken *them* so early in the morning. The Shevvingtons with their eyes like mad dogs? They would froth at the mouth and bite Christina if they did not get eight hours of sleep.

Two other island children were finishing out the school year boarding at the Inne: Michael and Benjamin Jaye, who were older, both in high school. Michael and Benj slept through anything. You would have to drop cement blocks on their feet to

3

waken them at dawn. No worry that they would get up and ask what she was doing, playing with fire.

She did worry about the stairs. Twisting, open, lined with a forest of fragile white banisters, they creaked with age. On the second-floor balcony, carpet began: thick, rich carpet that soaked up sound and warmed bare feet.

She crept past the Shevvingtons' bedroom. They had a lovely suite. The island children were kept in attic rooms with only a coat of paint to brighten them up.

Criminals have better housing than we do, thought Christina.

Behind their door, she heard the Shevvingtons talking. Mrs. Shevvington was her English teacher and Mr. Shevvington the high school principal. Christina flattened herself against the wall. If she had awakened them, school would not be worth living through. She listened to their voices, furry like leopards. They were talking of something else entirely.

". . . sell the Inne," said Mrs. Shevvington. Her voice was thick and sucking, like the mudflats at low tide. "We should get an excellent price for it. From city people who think it would be fun to run a bed and breakfast."

Christina nearly laughed. Mr. and Mrs. Shevvington did many things with those eight pretty bedrooms, but not once had they had a living guest.

No. These guest rooms held only the shells of the past.

". . . list it with a realtor today," said Mr. Shevvington. "I've been accepted as principal in that Chicago high school."

Christina pictured him: elegant and lean. Probably even his pajamas were tailored and impressive. All the parents adored Mr. Shevvington. They quoted him as if he were *The New York Times*. Even after all the terrible things that had happened that year, the parents still were on the Shevvingtons' side. "They tried their best," the grown-ups said sympathetically, bringing casseroles instead of drumming the Shevvingtons out of town.

Even Christina's mother and father said, "They were only trying to help their son, Chrissie. Have some compassion." For the Shevvingtons' grown son had been found living in Schooner Inne's cellar, giggling to himself, coming and going at low tide through the opening in the rock cliff.

People were already forgetting about Anya and Dolly.

Anya . . . Christina had always wanted to be and look just like Anya. Anya was very fair, and never tanned. Like a princess in a fairy tale, Anya remained chalk-white, with a frame of black hair so thick and heavy its weight curled her slender neck forward like a swan's. Anya had been the academic star of Burning Fog, the one everybody expected would go out into the world and bring fame to her family. Her boyfriend was a preppy townie named Blake, who dressed in what the children called Catalog Maine: rugby shirt, boat shoes without socks, loose trousers made of imported cotton. But then the Shevvingtons chose Anya, and bit by bit, turned Anya's senior year — which should have been a sort of heaven — into insanity, taking away her grades, her looks, and finally, Blake.

Next they chose Dolly, the youngest of the island children boarding at Schooner Inne. Dolly was elementary school size: a fragile collection of slender bones in big overalls, her red braids nearly as wide as her shoulders. They turned Dolly from a laughing, flying sixth-grader into a trembling, nervous creature sure that life would suffocate her; and sure enough, Dolly nearly had fatal accidents . . . three times.

How close the Shevvingtons had come to their goal — two island children destroyed in one school year. But Dolly was back on the island with her parents for the rest of the school year, and Anya had left for the city to stay with understanding relatives of Blake's.

So people were able to set the horror aside. They had a handy person to blame things on: the crazy son. Now that he was locked up it would be tacky and tasteless to mention the "problem" again.

"The Shevvingtons," everybody informed Christina, "have suffered enough."

As if Christina had not suffered! As if Anya and Dolly had not suffered!

". . . beautifully cleaned up," said Mrs. Shevvington. "I'll light fires in all the fireplaces when buyers come to look. It will seem so homey and cozy with embers glowing."

Homey! Cozy! The Shevvingtons? Hah!

And then Christina truly listened . . . the words sank into her sleepy, crack-of-dawn brain. *The Shevvingtons were leaving town!* Putting Schooner Inne on the market!

She was free! She was safe!

Christina skimmed down the last flight of stairs, light as a tern. She slid barefoot out the front door and sat on the granite steps to put on her shoes. She stuck the can and candle behind the stone planter in which windbeaten geraniums struggled for life. The sun curled on her lap like a honey-colored dog, licking her with yellow warmth.

Christina began laughing. Life was good. She was soon to be fourteen; seventh grade was nearly over; the Shevvingtons were leaving town. What more could a girl ask for?

Mr. and Mrs. Shevvington also dressed early. Then, smiling softly, they walked into each guest room. They stroked the bright blue colors in one room and gloated over the soft yellows in another. Downstairs they paced through the beautiful parlors still decorated as the sea captain had fixed

7

them for his bride so many years before.

Nearly every room had a fireplace. These were not big sturdy brick fireplaces where colonial women cooked stew. They were small and elegant, surrounded by imported tiles and mantels of sea-green marble.

In the front parlor, the Shevvingtons crumpled newspaper, stacked kindling, and rested slender logs on the andirons. Mr. Shevvington struck a match. It was a wooden kitchen match. The big old house was drafty. The flame quivered, thin as a thread, and then fattened up, solid gold.

"I heard Christina go out," he remarked. His fingers were long and thin, like fireplace pokers.

"Christina," said Mrs. Shevvington dreamily, "would make a good wharf rat, don't you think?" She smiled, her little teeth like yellow corn, dried on the cob.

Mr. Shevvington laughed. His laugh crept through cracks like January winds. "Yes," he said. "A wharf rat. A girl who works on the docks, knee-deep in fish heads and motor oil, and loses all her teeth before she's twenty-five."

"A girl who sits alone eating jelly doughnuts, getting fat and repulsive, and nobody cares," added Mrs. Shevvington.

"A wharf rat," they said together.

Fire licked the wood, stretching into the chimney, reaching for oxygen. Silver and gold flames consumed the brown logs. "The three colors," said Mr. Shevvington, "of Christina's hair." His eyes were soft and warm, like a baby blanket.

Mrs. Shevvington's yellowish eyes were like poached eggs in an oatmeal face. "We do have," she said, "eighteen more days."

"How nice," said Mr. Shevvington.

Chapter 2

Late that afternoon, the other seventh-graders on the beach began to think of supper instead of hacking around. They called their mothers from the public phone and got rides home. Christina watched enviously as mothers beeped their horns, calling, "Hi, honey, have a good time?"

I have a mother like that, she thought. But my mother's on the island.

She looked out to sea. Burning Fog Isle was lost in the thick fog that had started rolling in. Sometimes a trick of atmosphere occurred: The sun shone behind the fog, blazing like flames. Many times in the last three hundred years, mainlanders had rushed to save ships at sea or houses on the Isle from fire. But there never was a real fire; it was just the fog, catching the sun in its soft gray prism.

Christina loved the fog. It hugged her and kept her secrets. It belonged to the sea and went back to the sea; and you could neither hold it nor summon it.

The wind fingered her hair, until it was a mass of gold-and-silver ribbons. She walked alone up Breakneck Hill. The quick-moving fog walked with her, wrapping her like a wet scarf. Unlocking the heavy green door, she let herself into the gloom of the front hall of Schooner Inne. The only light came from the cupola three stories up. The paper on the wall was flocked and formal; nobody would ever crayon on those walls, or even lean against them. She passed the parlor where nobody ever sat, for the chairs were stiff and sharp, and the sofas rigid and unwelcoming.

In the fireplace was a silent fire.

Christina blinked, backed up, and looked in the door again.

Fire glittered. But it made no crackle, gave off no scent, produced no smoke. Christina moved toward the fire like an iron filing slithering toward a magnet. She stretched out her fingers for warmth but felt none.

A fire without heat.

Hair falling forward, blending with the flames, Christina bent to touch the cold fire.

An odd catlike smell filled the room.

Mrs. Shevvington's voice purred. She said, "Christina, darling, what is this fascination you have with fire?"

Christina jumped. There was something subhuman about the way Mrs. Shevvington could appear anywhere, like an ant or a mouse coming through the cracks unheard.

Behind Mrs. Shevvington stood the brothers, Michael and Benj. Michael was growing so fast you could hardly keep track of him; he was fifteen now, and getting muscular, his favorite cotton sweater shoved up past the elbow. He had cut his hair even shorter, as if the taller he got, the less hair he needed. Benj was just solid; Benj had always seemed like a grown-up. He had skipped childhood entirely. His face rarely divided into smiles or frowns. Christina always wanted Benj to shout and laugh. But Benj was just there.

Mrs. Shevvington said, "I've not forgotten that dreadful episode during the winter, Christina, when you set fire to your clothes."

Christina sucked in her breath. She hated looking at Mrs. Shevvington. Sideways, the woman had no profile.

In his heavy voice, dragging like a net on the bottom of the sea, Benj said, "Mrs. Shevvington, we all know it was your son who set that fire."

Christina nearly fell over. Benjamin was defending her?

Mrs. Shevvington's eyes grew dark and threatening, like a thunderstorm. But Benj was too solid for her. She went snarling back into the kitchen.

"Benj," said Christina delightedly, "you stuck up for me."

"You saved my sister Dolly's life, didn't you," he said, without a question mark at the end, as if Benj did not have questions, only facts.

"Yes, I did," she said. For it was a fact. She had

thought everyone had forgotten the terrible night in which she dragged Dolly across the mudflats, desperately trying to reach the opposite shore, while the tide hurtled forward to claim their bodies, and take them out to sea forever. While the Shevvingtons' insane son stood on the ledge, ready to throw them back into the sea if they tried to go back into Schooner Inne. Sometimes at night she woke to the sound of his laughter, shrieking over the waves, and she was never quite sure if it was a nightmare — or his return by dark.

It was nice to have done a good deed, and even nicer to get credit for that moment of courage that kept Dolly alive. Christina bounced toward old Benj, feeling warm toward him, warm toward the world. "Benjamin, Ice Cream Delight opened for the season. After supper do you want to go there and get a sundae with me?"

Benjamin stared at her incredulously. You would have thought he had never in his life gone for ice cream. He was too amazed even to answer her and went on in to supper.

Christina paused to check the silent fire. It was crinkled Mylar paper. Yellow, orange, and scarlet paper cut into flame shapes, crushed down over black Mylar that gleamed like coals. Fire of foil. How well done it was. And how like the Shevvingtons, she thought, to think that a fake fire will be cozy and homey enough for all those prospective Inne buyers.

She laughed to herself. She was always giving

the Shevvingtons credit for supernatural abilities. And there always turned out to be dull explanations. Like the changing poster of the sea that had driven Anya crazy, its evil, curling waves beckoning her over the edge one day, and the next day its painted ocean flat and wall-poster blue. Eventually they found out that Mrs. Shevvington just switched two posters back and forth.

Christina went into the kitchen with the others. They never ate in the dining room, always in the kitchen, on a hideously ugly table, its top chipped, its legs as fat as thighs. Benj was setting the table.

He's sixteen and they already call him Old Benj, thought Christina. He'll quit high school and be a lobsterman like his father and grandfather before him, and he won't say another syllable unless he's forced to. I wonder how he'll ask a girl to marry him? Perhaps she'll ask him. Then all he'll have to do is nod.

Christina plopped down in her chair.

"Christina," said Mr. Shevvington, "sit gracefully. Do not just let go and fall into the chair."

Christina tried to decide whether this was worth a fight or not. There were any number of arguments about sitting techniques.

But Benj said, "I think she is graceful." Benjamin passed the creamed potatoes Christina's way.

Christina hated sauces. There was something sinister about them, whether they were milk-white, hollandaise-yellow, spinach-green, or tomato-red. They hid the true food. You could not be sure what those little chopped things were, down at the bottom of the sauce. It hadn't been so bad when Dolly and Anya still lived there. Anya could always be counted on to surface from her foggy world to identify lumps for Christina. "That's an onion. That's a mushroom." (Dolly never ate anyway, her skinny little arms and legs barely stapled to her body. So it hadn't mattered to Dolly.)

How Christina missed Anya! Anya was as beautiful as sea foam, her thick dark hair a cloud around her translucent skin. But Anya had had no strength. Not like me, thought Christina with satisfaction. I'm like the Isle: I'm granite. Behind the safe cover of her tilted milk glass, Christina sneered at the Shevvingtons. It felt pretty good.

"Guess what," said Benjamin Jaye.

Christina choked on her milk. "Since when have you ever told us anything at all," she asked him, "let alone said to guess at it?"

Benjamin grinned at her.

Even the Shevvingtons blinked at the sight of Benj grinning.

"Is that a grin?" Christina teased.

Benjamin grinned even wider.

"You know how!" she cried. "Benj! You're so cute when you grin."

Now he blushed.

His younger brother said, "This is disgusting. Stop it, Benj. Just tell them."

Benj said, "The marching band is going to Disney World next fall. All we have to do is raise the money for forty-four of us to make the trip, and we get to be the Disney World band for the day! *Me.*"

"Oh, Benjamin!" Christina screamed. "Florida? You'll fly down? In those wonderful band uniforms! All scarlet and gold braid, and white shoes. All those years of playing the trumpet are finally paying off. That's so great!"

Benjamin, who had possibly the world's largest appetite, was too excited to eat. Christina had never come across a boy who could not eat. Benj kept filling his fork and then setting it back down on the plate, untouched. "We'll take a bus down to Orlando," he said. "Flying's too expensive. But a really nice bus, with a bathroom and a snack bar. We'll stay five days."

"Five days at Disney World," breathed Christina. "That is so wonderful, Benj. You'll have the best time. How much money do we have to raise? I'll help. You'll need tons. Millions. We'll have car washes and bake sales and hike-a-thons."

Mr. Shevvington said, "At this point, the school has not yet given permission."

Benj dropped his fork, his face speaking instead of his tongue. *You might refuse to let us go to Disney World?*

Christina glared at Mr. Shevvington. "You won't even be here next year," she said hotly, forgetting she had learned this by eavesdropping. "You're getting a job in another state. So there."

"It won't matter if they have permission or not,"

said Mrs. Shevvington. "They can't raise that kind of money. A scrubby little Maine village like this? Hah!" she sniffed. "Don't set your heart on it, Benjamin, because it will not come about."

"Anyway," said Michael, his mouth all pouty, "why should everybody raise all that money for just you guys? Forty-four of you get to go to Disney World, but we don't. I don't play an instrument. So why should I help?"

Christina was outraged. "Because he's your brother," she said. "You're mean, Michael. You've been getting all the glory all year with your games and your trophies. Now you don't want your own brother to have any?"

Michael said, "He doesn't work as hard as we did. Band is just a dumb class, like art or cooking. Athletic teams have to practice every day after school. And Saturdays. What do they have to do for Band? Just show up, is all."

The brothers glared at each other.

Mrs. Shevvington said, "You're right, Michael. Benjamin rarely practices. And of course, he doesn't make that much of a contribution to the band anyway. After all these years, he's only third trumpet."

Benj, on whose face emotion so rarely showed, flinched. He stared down into his creamed potatoes so he would not have to see his brother's jealous eyes and the Shevvingtons' cruel mouths.

Christina thought, So that's what they'll do these last eighteen days. Try to hurt everybody in sight.

Look how quickly they stabbed old Benj. First time he's ever been filled with joy, and they punctured him right away.

Benjamin tried to take a sip from his glass, failed, and put it back on the table. The glass shook.

"You don't feel well," observed Mrs. Shevvington, a tiny smile slitting her face.

Benj shrugged.

"Seconds please," said Michael, pointing toward the serving bowls.

"Eat what Benj left on his plate," suggested Christina, "since you're the one who spoiled his appetite."

"Christina!" said Mrs. Shevvington. "Your manners are deteriorating every day. I am appalled at you. Go to your room."

"No," said Christina. "Benj and I are going for ice cream." She stood up, heart pounding. Disobeying the Shevvingtons was scary. She did not look at their eyes. His would be glittering like a seagull's, as it swept down to peck open a tern's egg. Hers would be little stones, as if there were not a person inside; just gravel.

"Your fourteenth birthday is only a few weeks away," said Mr. Shevvington, "and you are behaving like a spoiled toddler."

Benj said, "I forgot about your birthday, Chrissie. That's neat. It's hard to believe you'll be fourteen."

That was so much speech coming from Benj she

felt they should write it down and save it for his grandchildren to read.

"We should do something special," added Benj. "Since your mom and dad can't give you a party until you get back to the island for summer." He touched his jeans pocket where his wallet made a rectangular bulge. Benj worked at the gas station and saved every cent toward the new motor he wanted for his boat. It had not occurred to Christina that he would pay for the ice cream. She had expected to use her allowance.

If he paid, it would be like a date.

She hid her giggle at the mere idea of Benjamin having a date.

"I'm coming for ice cream, too," said Michael, jealous over even a tiny thing his brother might have and he wouldn't. "We'll try to think of something for Christina's birthday."

Mrs. Shevvington's smile was horrid, her little yellow teeth lined up like broken candy. She purred, "Perhaps *we* can think of something to do with Christina."

Chapter 3

Christina, in the middle, was by far the smallest. Her tri-colored hair flew in the wind like flags.

Michael was on her right. He talked loudly of sports and teams. She had never noticed before that Michael was something of a spoiled brat. Look at him, she thought. He can't bear it that Benj would even have an ice-cream cone that he doesn't have, let alone Disney World. And he certainly isn't going to let anybody talk about my birthday.

Mrs. Shevvington's words battered her head. *Perhaps we can think of something to do with Christina.* It did not sound like parties and confetti; it sounded like doom and destruction. She kept thinking of that creepy candle in the coffee can.

Benjamin was on her left. She came up to his shoulder. And what a shoulder it was. Curving muscle burst out from below the T-shirt, threatening to split the cotton. Benj, who never talked, talked steadily — right through his brother's babble, as if they were unaware of each other. He talked of Epcot and Space Mountain and his marching band uniform.

Behind them came the Shevvingtons, who had decided that they, too, needed a first ice cream of the season.

The five of us look like a family, Christina thought. People who don't know us would think What an interesting set of parents, what beautiful children.

That was enough to make her lose her appetite for ice cream. The idea of being Christina Shevvington instead of Christina Romney! "Yuck," she said out loud.

"You don't like the band uniforms?" said Benj.

"You don't think I'm the best ball player?" said Michael.

They were on the sidewalk, going down the treacherous rim of Breakneck Hill. Below them the tide slithered into Candle Cove like a muddy pancake, and then, hitting the rocks, spewed violently, like a pancake being whipped in a blender. The highest tides in Maine occurred in this very cove. Every few years, the tide picked an ignorant summer person off the rocks, or caught him in the mudflats, and sometimes the body was found and sometimes it wasn't.

Christina shivered, although the evening was hot. What will the Shevvingtons do with me? she thought. Will I be found? Here she was with two strapping boys who liked her — and neither one would believe it if she said the Shevvingtons were plotting against her. They were too busy thinking of baseball and Florida. She wrenched her mind off cliffs and drowning, fires and candles. "It's such a terrible decision what kind of ice cream to get, don't you think?" she babbled. "I love vanilla. I love chocolate. But each year they kick off the season with a new flavor, and it would be criminal not to taste it."

"Criminal, Chrissie?" Benjamin considered her word carefully. "It's not that severe."

"She's exaggerating, Benj," explained Michael, making his brother sound stupid. "That's what Christina does best anyhow. Stretch a story to fit."

The Shevvingtons laughed. "That's true, Michael. Christina tells more yarns than anybody in Maine."

Christina knotted her fist. She felt like appeasing the appetite of the tide with Shevvington bodies.

"There's a solution to your ice-cream problem, Chrissie," explained Michael in a condescending voice. "It's pretty high-tech. That's why you never thought of it. Just get a three-scoop cone." He laughed at her.

Christina's fist came straight up to Michael's nose, but he had grown up with her, and he was ready for it. He caught both her wrists, disarming her as easily as he would a toddler. He laughed. "No point in struggling, Chrissie," he said. "I'm a hundred times stronger."

His fingers closed around her wrists like locks.

She scrabbled at him, trying to get free. Nothing happened.

"Michael, you are so strong," said Mrs. Shevvington, full of admiration. "Why, you could toss Christina over the cliff as easily as an empty lunch bag." The wind tore her chuckle out of her mouth and tossed it into the sea.

Empty. It was the Shevvingtons' word. That was what they did to their victims. They emptied them. Emptied their bodies, and put their souls to rest forever in the silent guest rooms of Schooner Inne.

Christina struggled. She felt like a little animal, a kitten dragged to the vet — to be held down for shots — to be put to sleep forever.

Michael will be their instrument, she thought. That's how they'll do it to me. Mrs. Shevvington isn't going to let these eighteen days go unused.

Benjamin had his brother in a wrestling lock. "Let go," Benj said, for whom two words would always be enough. Michael's fingers went limp. Christina was free.

"My goodness but you're prickly, Benjamin," said Mrs. Shevvington. "Can't you take a joke?"

Benjamin glared at Mrs. Shevvington. If her eyes were pebbles, his were boulders. Suddenly Christina felt herself sister to Benj. They were carved of the same granite, from the same quarry, from the same island in the sea. "Come on, Benj," she said, grabbing his hand, "let's get there first."

* * *

In the morning, Benjamin did not stride off to school by himself but waited for Christina. She was astounded. Last summer the brothers had informed her in no uncertain terms that friendship must be left back on Burning Fog Isle; she must not expect them to associate with a lowly seventh-grader. She of course had tagged after them anyway, until they growled, "Christina, buzz off."

Today, the sun came up like a trumpet announcing *summer! Summer! Summer!*

And Benjamin Jaye held the heavy green door open for Christina, and shortened his big strides to match hers. The wind tugged her tri-colored hair, separating it. This was a good sign. (Christina never read horoscopes. She listened to her hair.) "You really want me to help with the fund-raising, don't you, Benj? I promise I will. You don't have to walk with me. Anyway, I'm meeting Jonah at the gate."

Benj said nothing, but she had not expected him to. They walked on. Such a glorious day! She was wearing a pretty cotton dress, with a tulip-flared skirt in watered pastels. She even had a new purse, nubby cotton, all fat and sagging and full of her own things. She loved purses. They were sacred. People might say how pretty your purse was, but they never went into your purse. You could have secrets in it if you wanted. "You know what I was thinking last night?" said Christina. She hoped for a syllable, but Benj raised both eyebrows instead. "At least it's a two-eyebrow morning," she teased him.

He laughed.

"I was thinking that for Disney World, we'll need grown-up money, not kid money," explained Christina. "We need to do things that attract tourists. They're the ones with the money. Now listen up. Clam chowder is the town specialty."

"Lobster is," Benj corrected her.

"Lobster, too, but listen. I need clams."

They were at the gate, and there was Jonah. Jonah was sort of Christina's boyfriend. Nobody in seventh grade actually had a boyfriend, but Jonah was a boy, and he liked her a lot, and sometimes they said they were "going together."

"Clams?" said Jonah. He poked Benj in the chest. "Well, you got one, Chrissie." He laughed hysterically.

Benjamin took Jonah's extended finger and began to snap it off. "Benj!" said Christina, getting between them. What could have made Jonah — a scrawny thirteen-year-old — start something with Benj, who could have modeled for a gym-equipment ad?

"I don't like clam or lobster jokes," said Benj. "Just because I keep silent when there's nothing to say, Jonah, doesn't mean I'm a crustacean."

Christina looked at the pair of them. How obvious the age difference was! Jonah was actually slightly taller than Benj, having grown like a stilt all winter. But he was skinny, with a lopsided, loping bounce. Benj's arms were twice as thick. His tan had never faded because he worked year round at the sea and at the gas station. He already had a lobsterman's squint, from the sun glaring off the water. It did not seem that two and a half years separated the boys; it seemed like ten.

"Anyway," Benj prompted her. He ignored Jonah, as sixteen-year-olds always ignored seventh-grade boys.

"Anyway, I think we could get all the restaurants in town to donate a vat of their own special recipe of clam chowder. We could set it up at the wharf. Decorate each dock like a particular restaurant. And people could buy a ticket and taste twenty kinds of chowder."

"Yuck," said Jonah. "I hate clam chowder."

"Nobody cares about you," said Christina. "It's tourists we're interested in. We need money so Benj can go to Disney World."

Jonah rolled his eyes. "Christina," he said, just as Michael had, "that's the high school. Who cares? It's their problem whether they can raise the money. Do you know how much time and effort it would take to do that chowder thing? Let them raise their own money. Besides, you couldn't do that till July or August when tourists are really here, and you'll be out on that island of yours." He made Burning Fog Isle sound like a garbage dump.

Her island of wild grass and roses, of salt spray and seabirds floating? Christina lowered her head as if to batter Jonah to his senses. Nobody got away with saying bad things about Burning Fog when Christina Romney was alive to stop them. Jonah dashed off with a bunch of boys who were climbing up on the school roof to retrieve the mittens, tennis balls, and book reports thrown there during the year. "I'll get you later!" yelled Christina. Jonah, safe on the roof, lay down on the shingles and shrugged.

Benjamin took a breath as if to ask Christina something. The wind suddenly ripped in from the sea, and a whiff of low tide filled their noses. Christina's cotton dress whirled up. She caught the hem, and from her windblown pocket fell a book of matches.

"What's this?" said Benjamin, frowning. "Christina, you're not experimenting with smoking cigarettes, are you?"

"Of course not. Don't be dumb. Those aren't my matches. They must have been on the pavement."

Benjamin gave her a strange look. "Chowder's a good idea," he mumbled, and walked away.

What was that all about? thought Christina.

"Christina," came a whisper.

She looked around, seeing nobody. There were dozens of kids outside because the bell hadn't rung yet. Why would anybody whisper?

"*Christina!*" it hissed.

She shivered. It sounded like the tide calling her name. That was what Anya thought, Christina remembered, when she was going mad. *The sea is a mathematician*, Anya had cried; *the sea keeps count, the sea wants one of us.*

Anya had been entranced by the tides. *Listen,*

she would whisper, her long fingers holding Christina like a net holding fish under water. *The tide is saying, "Come! Come here and drown with me!"*

A cloud covered the sun.

The trumpet-gold day turned to shadows.

Christina shivered uncontrollably.

A damp cold finger touched her neck, and she screamed, leaping backward.

It was only Robbie. Ordinary old Robbie Armstrong from English class. "Robbie, you scared me," she accused him, panting for breath. "I dropped my purse." Why am I so jumpy? she thought. A minute ago I was happy.

Her scream had drawn attention. A strange, silent, serious attention. Eyes stared at Christina — and at the ground around her.

On the pavement, where children of another generation had painted hopscotch lines, lay a dozen books of matches. Her cloth purse was not as fat as it had been: all those matchbooks had spurted out when the purse hit the ground.

The principal had been standing on the school steps, waiting for the warning bell to summon the children to class. Now Mr. Shevvington walked down the wide granite slabs, his polished black shoes clapping like hands against the rock. He was very tall. Christina had to look way up into his face. The sun was behind him, flooding her eyes, so she had to duck her head. Mr. Shevvington pointed to the match pile. "Christina," he said into the listening silence. "What have you been setting fire to?"

Chapter 4

Twenty people heard.

They each told their friends.

By lunch, the entire school had heard. *Mr. Shevvington says Christina Romney's been setting fire to things. You should have seen all the matches she had. But you know what those island girls are like. Remember when Anya tried to push Blake over the cliff into the tide? Oh, they tried to blame it all on the Shevvingtons' son, but still . . . when things like this happen . . . you wonder.*

In the cafeteria Vicki and Gretch smirked. They told the story of the match pile again, making it bigger, more convincing, and scarier.

"What were all your matches for?" Jonah asked her.

"They weren't mine. Mrs. Shevvington must have stuffed them in my purse."

"I told you," said Jonah, in the voice people always use with that sentence. A nyah-nyah voice.

"I told you something was going to happen, but did you listen to me? No. You ran off with Old Benj."

Several kids giggled, as if Old Benj were a well-known joke among them.

"Honestly, Chrissie," Jonah went on. "You want to be a wharf rat? Married at sixteen, have ten kids, make fishnets all winter, and get gray hair?"

"I will not be a wharf rat," said Christina fiercely. "And neither will Benj." Her fists doubled up under the cafeteria table. Don't get into a fight, she told herself. You don't have to defend Benjamin Jaye. He can defend himself.

"Then why are you hanging around him, all lovey-dovey like that?" demanded Jonah.

"Lovey-dovey?" cried Christina. "Jonah, get a grip on yourself. He's like my brother."

Jonah snorted. *"You* get a grip on *your*self," he said. "He's going to quit school, he won't be back for junior year. He'll ask you to marry him, and you will."

"I'm fourteen!" shouted Christina, rounding off a few weeks.

"So? Big deal. He's sixteen. What's two years? My father is eleven years older than my mother." Jonah folded his arms across his chest as if he had just won an important argument.

Mrs. Shevvington walked into the cafeteria. She never did that. She did not have a free period when the seventh grade had lunch. She looked around the cafeteria, her eyes roving inside her one-dimensional face, like movable eyes in an oil painting.

Her eyes seemed to cut Christina out of the crowd like a sheep dog isolating one of his flock.

The cafeteria was filled with sunlight and the laughter of others. Other people split Oreo cookies, one taking the filling and one the chocolate side. Other people handed around Doritos and brownies. Other people discussed with Jonah whether or not in the state of Maine you could get married as young as Chrissie and Benj were. But for Christina, participation ceased. Something is here, something has come, she thought. But what?

Slow as low tide, Mrs. Shevvington drifted over to Christina. She touched Christina's cheek. Her finger pad was mushy as a jellyfish dying on the rocks. "Christina," said Mrs. Shevvington. Lovingly, for the benefit of her audience. To other people the Shevvingtons always seemed to be the good ones. "Mr. Shevvington is quite worried about you, dear. Do you want to discuss something with me?"

I want to throw you off Breakneck Hill, thought Christina.

But for once she was wise enough to stay silent.

"Mr. Shevvington thinks you are smoking cigarettes. He thinks that's why you carry a purse full of matches. But I am afraid it's more serious than that, isn't it, Christina?" Mrs. Shevvington nodded her head, like a guillotine in slow motion. "Because you don't need a dozen books of matches for one cigarette, do you, Christina?"

Across the cafeteria Vicki hissed, "Chrissie's done something terrible! I bet she's gone mad, the way island girls do!"

Christina was usually alert during English class, but today she was anesthetized by what had happened to her. She could not seem to hear what was going on. Every time she looked up she snagged on Mrs. Shevvington's eyes. Christina could not feel herself inside her dress; she was the dress; she was nothing but a piece of cotton. She could not feel her hair: The three colors had withered away. There was nothing now to protect her.

All I have to do is hang on, Christina told herself. They have only seventeen days now, and what can they do in such a short time? If I stay calm, and don't play into their hands, I'll be all right.

"We will want to have a class party, of course," said Mrs. Shevvington, "to celebrate the end of school."

Everybody wanted a party. Even people who had had a terrible school year wanted a party.

"We'll have it at my aunt's summer house," Vicki commanded. Vicki was wealthy, and never lost an opportunity to say so. Her aunt owned a house right on the ocean, one of the few with actual sand rather than rocks and cliffs. The beach was only a few yards wide, but you could spread a towel on it. Maybe two or three towels. Above the beach was a wide meadow, and there they could play volleyball, softball, and Frisbee.

"How generous of you, Vicki, dear," said Mrs. Shevvington. She was sticky, like the back of a stamp. She caught children to her: first their eyes, later their souls. The smile searched the room like a fisherman trolling. The children ducked their heads, staring into the corners of the room, or down into their laps. They all had their own ways of avoiding the smile.

It was Robbie that the smile caught today. It changed his posture, made his breathing ragged. His thin, little boy's chest plopped nervously up and down.

"Robbie," said Mrs. Shevvington, in her cruel, teasing voice, "I will put you in charge of organizing the class party."

"*I* want to be in charge!" cried Vicki. "It's on my aunt's beach."

"I think Robbie has hidden qualities of leadership," said Mrs. Shevvington. Her lips were thin as pencil lead. She drew a smile with her pencil lips and laughed. "Well-hidden qualities, of course."

Robbie flinched.

"But we want to encourage Robbie, don't we, class?" said Mrs. Shevvington. "We want to bring out his best, don't we?" Her sticky eyes absorbed their snickering laughter. "Come to the front of the class, Robbie."

They all knew Robbie hated standing up alone; he couldn't talk once their faces stared at him; his cheek would twitch. It would not bring out his best. It would destroy him.

Destroy, Christina thought.

For a terrible, selfish moment she was glad that the smile had caught Robbie and not her.

"Oh, Mrs. Shevvington," Vicki pouted. "He can't do anything right. It'll all be spoiled."

"That's been true in the past," Mrs. Shevvington agreed. "But every student of mine should have many chances." Her eyes ceased to blink. They narrowed; they pierced Robbie like Indian arrowheads. Slowly Robbie got out of his chair. Mrs. Shevvington's eyes hauled him past Vicki, past Gretch, up to the front of the class. Two dozen pairs of eyes watched him now. "Don't shuffle, Robbie," said Mrs. Shevvington. "You look like a second-grader who needs to be excused."

Robbie flushed an ugly mottled purple.

The class tilted toward Christina, waiting for her to stand up for Robbie, the way she always did. Christina avoided their eyes. How many times have I gotten involved? she thought. Complained to my parents, told other kids' parents, let the guidance office know what she's like. Don't you see how Mrs. Shevvington undermines us, and lays traps for us, and lets us bleed in front of everybody? I say to them. But the grown-ups always say, Christina, why must you always exaggerate? Why must you tell so many yarns? Mrs. Shevvington is trying to build your self-esteem; she's a fine teacher; you just have a bad attitude.

Christina ignored Robbie. She pretended to study her English book. There on the inside cover were penciled doodles. Candles, flames, and the tips of matches. A shiver took possession of Christina's spine and slithered over her tanned skin. She could not remember drawing those. She usually doodled tic-tac-toes.

Fire, she thought. The candle. Did I — ? No, I couldn't have. I don't do things like that.

Mrs. Shevvington's little black eyes abandoned Robbie; they focused on Christina; a smile like fungus on a rotted log grew out of Mrs. Shevvington's thin lips. Christina traced the fire doodles with her finger.

Robbie's cheek jerked. He wet his lips.

"Robbie's older sister was also weak," said Mrs. Shevvington, her eyes centering on Christina. "It's in the family genes. Val Armstrong had to be institutionalized."

Christina was the only seventh-grader with courage. She thought it was because of her island upbringing. She was granite, Christina of the Isle. Any other day, she would have retorted, "*Your* son had to be institutionalized, too, you know, Mrs. Shevvington. Your genes are nothing to brag about, either. You only said that to be mean."

But today she could not worry about Robbie, or his sister Val. For she could not get her mind off fire. She saw the flames on which they would roast hot dogs and the coals over which they would toast marshmallows. Vaguely she heard Vicki take over the picnic organization, after it was agreed that Robbie was too stupid; remotely she saw Robbie creep back to his seat. Gretch and Vicki discussed the menu. Suddenly it seemed very important to arrange for the bonfire. What if Vicki and Gretch forgot about the beach fire?

Christina interrupted. "First of all," she said urgently, "we'll need a huge fire. We should start gathering driftwood right now for the bonfire."

"A fire comes first?" repeated Mrs. Shevvington. Her f's and her s's hissed and curled like snakes. *A ffffire comesssss ffffirsssssst.* "How interesting, Christina. You have a special interest in fire, don't you?"

Christina nodded. "I love fire," she agreed. "Our bonfire should have flames up to the sky." She imagined craggy boulders, the bonfire thrusting among them, framed against the sky and the sea. She smiled to herself.

Mrs. Shevvington's eyes grew like puddles in a flood. *"Fffflames up to the ssssssky."* she repeated. She turned to the class. "Say it with me," she told them, and they said it with her, like some horrible rhyme: *A ffffire comesssss ffffirsssssst . . . Fffflames up to the ssssssky . . . Chhhrrrisssssstina lovesssss ffffffire. . . .*

Mrs. Shevvington's eyes glittered like flecks of mica on rocks. In her furry voice, rasping like a cat's tongue on soft skin, she whispered, "There have been several suspicious fires in town lately, haven't there, class?"

Chapter 5

As a hiker in the woods checks herself for ticks, for the rest of the school day Christina searched herself continually for matches. She would never again wear clothes with pockets. She would stop carrying a purse. That would foil them.

The nerve of them! Sneaking into Christina's room, touching her clothes, fingering her pockets, stuffing her handbag, starting rumors!

And they'll laugh, she thought, because I knew all along and never could convince anybody. Every terrible thing that happened they weaseled out of because they could use their own son to blame it on! That bonfire last winter, when my whole wardrobe was burned in the snow — when everybody blamed me and said I was going island-mad. It was them, I know it was them.

Twice now — at least — the Shevvingtons had skulked through Christina's room, opened her drawers, handled her clothing, played tricks with fire and matches.

They got Anya by working on her fears, she thought. They won't do it that way with me. They won't try to make *me* afraid. They'll use rumor. They'll arrange my world so that other people become afraid of me.

At the end of the day, Robbie, slinking down the hall like her shadow, crept up behind her. His fingers touched her like falling ice cubes. "Robbie," snapped Christina, "if you hadn't scared me out there — "

"Listen," hissed Robbie.

"Stop whispering. You sound like a snake. Nothing but s's."

Robbie said, "I'm going to visit my sister Val in the institution. You know, the mental home where Mr. and Mrs. Shevvington talked my parents into putting her? The social worker has to visit a bunch of patients there this afternoon, and he said he'd take me along tomorrow after school. You want to come?"

Val, Val, who was crimson and blue.

Last winter, being punished for something she had not done, Christina had been confined alone in Schooner Inne. And that day, peeking into the empty guest rooms that ringed the tilting balcony, she understood why Mr. and Mrs. Shevvington owned a guest house, but did not advertise nor accept guests. Each room was a victim. No flesh and blood would occupy those rooms. They were already occupied.

With ghosts.

The Shevvingtons had even furnished the rooms to match. That was one of their hobbies: admiring their guest rooms, cherishing the memories of their collection of empty girls.

Anya had been number 8; the room meant for her had been fragile like lace, its carpets and cushions streaked with silver and gray — like storm clouds.

Anya had been saved. Christina and Blake had accomplished that.

But Robbie Armstrong's sister, Val, whom the Shevvingtons had chosen the year before — Val had been lost.

Number 7 was Val. Carpet blue as the sea in summer, walls rich violet, like sunset. Dark like a crimson flower in a crystal vase. This was the living Val: Val before the Shevvingtons. And now Val was mindless on a narrow cot in a quiet hospital.

Or was she mindless? Would she have clues? Would she have knowledge? Would she be able to say to Christina, from the fragments of her left in the real world, *This is how to stop the Shevvingtons?*

Room 8, meant for Anya's ghost — stormy and fallen — could be redecorated. It could become Christina's, a room of fire and islands.

Seventeen days were enough.

The minute school was out, everybody converged on Vicki's aunt's beach to study the grounds and make the important decisions. Most of the girls stood around arguing about who would bring the volleyball net and who would supply the radios and cassette players. Most of the boys scoured the beach for logs, pieces of smashed boat, steps off dock ladders, and other debris. Christina forgot Mrs. Shevvington. She loved being outdoors. Anything to do with the beach and the sea was home to Christina.

Christina and Jonah climbed over seaweed-slippery rocks, dragging wood, until the pile was taller than any of them. "Now that," said Christina, surveying the mountain of wood, "will make a real fire."

"Ssssshhhhhh!" said Jonah. He looked around uneasily. "Don't talk so loud, you dumbo," he whispered.

"Why not?"

"Didn't you see Mrs. Shevvington looking at you? Her eyes stuck to you like chewing gum, Chrissie. There may be only seventeen more days till the end of the school year," said Jonah, "but there's next year to worry about, too. Eighth grade. Think of all they could plan over the summer, Chrissie. Be careful."

Eighth grade. Room 8.

Did it mean something? Was it fate?

"The Shevvingtons don't scare me anymore," she said, which was a lie. "Besides, they won't be here next year. He's getting a job in Chicago, and they're putting Schooner Inne on the market." She looked down at the sand at her feet. She was foot-doodling. She often wrote her initials in the sand. But these were not initials. They were —

"Leaving?" repeated Jonah. He frowned. "But they have such a perfect setup here. The town adores them. They can get away with anything. Why would they leave?"

Candle flames. She had drawn fire. Was Mrs. Shevvington right? Who had drawn those English book doodles? The memory of the candle in the coffee can came back to her. Her own urgent voice saying fire had to come first.

Christina erased her sand marks. Her leg was shaking, as if she had just fallen or nearly had an accident. "Who cares?" she said. "They're going." Her head filled with candles and arson, with slippery cliffs and tumbling rocks.

Gretch was promising to bring a badminton set.

"Be sure to buy extra birdies," ordered Vicki. Vicki had a small notebook in which she was writing down everybody's promises. "See, Robbie," she said, "this is how it's done. When your hidden leadership qualities rise up, be sure to bring a notebook along."

This is what they had learned in seventh grade: how to taunt each other. Mrs. Shevvington treated the seventh-graders like pets. Dogs to be kicked — like Robbie. Dogs to be put on a leash — like Vicki. Vicki would do anything Mrs. Shevvington told her to.

Jennie said eagerly that she had a shiny new croquet set; she would bring her croquet set.

"Nobody wants to play croquet," said Vicki scornfully, "it's slow and pointless. Don't bring your old croquet set."

The delight vanished from Jennie's eyes. Shame replaced it. Jennie hung her head and scuffled her old sneakers in the sand.

Vicki and her best friend Gretch were "in." This was a phenomenon Christina had read about, but never experienced till this year, as the island had so few children. Seventh-graders angled for the chance to share a table with Vicki and Gretch. Vicki and Gretch were given extra desserts. Their opinions were sought and their jokes laughed at.

Now Jennie was the joke.

Fat, ugly Katy stepped up close to the important notebook. "I'll bring the marshmallows," she offered. "And I can cut plenty of green twigs to toast them on. We have lots of good bushes on our property."

Vicki smiled. She touched her own silk-smooth hair, admired her own slender ankles. "How suitable, Katy," she said, in the smooth, vicious voice she had learned from Mrs. Shevvington. "Marshmallows match your face."

Christina lost her temper. "I'll give *you* a marshmallow face!" she yelled. She hit Vicki.

Jonah pulled Christina off. "Don't give her a bloody lip," he said, "or you'll be in trouble again.

Less than three weeks to go, Chrissie. Stay good!"

"*I* don't get into trouble!" said Christina. How could her only ally talk like that? Jonah knew the truth; had always known the truth. "The Shevvingtons force me into it."

"Oh ho!" said Vicki. "Now you're going to blame poor Mr. and Mrs. Shevvington because you hit me. I'll tell you something, Christina Romney. Not everybody believes that the Shevvingtons' son did all the stuff you said he did." Vicki covered her swelling mouth with a manicured hand. "Like that time your entire winter wardrobe burned in a bonfire in the snow? You can't blame that on their son, Christina. We know better." Vicki raised her voice to reach her audience. "You're an island girl. They're all half crazy. You set that fire yourself."

The sea crept wetly around their sneakers, slurping at the dry land. The seventh grade watched Christina. It seemed to her that she was alone, and they were together; she was small and thin, and they were a crowd. A mob.

The force of their bodies and faces and eyes and voices rolled over her like a great drowning wave. Now they were a single creature: the enemy. A group to push her backward into Candle Cove and watch, laughing, while the tide came in over her broken bones.

Christina ran.

She had never done such a thing before. She was the fighter, the one who never gave up. Alone she ran, over the cliffs, among the craggy boulders, past the millionaires' mansions. Anything to get away, to be safe.

Her greatest fear in life was that she would be alone: without friends.

I should have given my friends a chance to speak up, she thought miserably. I played into the Shevvingtons' hands again. They want me friendless and running. And they've got it.

With her fists she rubbed away the tears that rolled over her eyes like fog over the island. So many victims. So much pain. All caused by Mr. and Mrs. Shevvington — humiliating, manipulating, taunting.

"But it doesn't matter now," Christina said to the sea gulls who floated in the air currents above her. "They're leaving!" she yelled to the barn swallows who dipped and swerved over the green meadow grass. "It's over!"

Christina went on past the old wharf that had once protruded a quarter mile into the ocean and was nothing now but piers sticking up like the feet of drowning men. She ran all the way to the storm cottages.

Many years before, in 1938, a great hurricane crossed New England. When it was over, buildings had been tossed to the ground in splinters. Back then, summer people came for only a few weeks, so they didn't care about quality building techniques. After the hurricane, the cottage owners made walls of broken boards and nailed on roofs that leaked and swayed.

The storm cottages looked as if they had been built with bent nails by a beginning Girl Scout troop. They tilted, with crazy stairs and mismatched windows. Some had plumbing and some didn't. Some had electricity and some didn't. It was hard to believe they were now worth hundreds of thousands of dollars because they were ocean-front.

Today, the storm cottages were still closed for the winter, shutters fastened over the windows.

Christina opened the shutters to the window on the sagging front porch of her favorite storm cottage. She eased the window up, and slipped inside. The storm cottage was painted white: ceilings, walls, doors, and even floors. The furniture was winter-draped in white sheets. A crack of sun came through the window Christina had opened, like a huge golden pencil.

Christina tiptoed through. In the funny old kitchen there were no counters, just a beaten-up table. The bathroom had a stand-up shower crammed in the corner, but the water was turned off. Upstairs a miniature bedroom held a bed with bare metal springs. Christina lay down and it was as comfortable as you would expect metal springs to be.

She knew these summer people. They came in August. And they did not rent it out the rest of the time. She could use the storm cottage for her hideout these last seventeen days. Actually, day seventeen was nearly over. Sixteen days, then. Who would hide out with me? she wondered.

Michael and Benjamin Jaye were the only other island children at Schooner Inne now.

On Burning Fog, Christina and Michael had been good friends, but the mainland pulled them apart. Michael was such a good athlete that he had already moved up the social ladder, and was important, because everybody knew he would be captain of everything one day, winning games against old rivals. Michael would laugh at her if she suggested a hideaway and Christina had been laughed at enough today.

Benjamin was out of the question. Benj was a sophomore, two years and six months older than Christina. If she told Benj about the storm cottage, the two years and six months between them would seem like a century. "Chrissie, that's trespassing," he would say in his heavy, slow, islander's voice.

"Not really," Christina would argue. "I've always done it. Besides, it's just a storm cottage. Practically public property."

Slowly a frown would materialize on Benj's forehead. Benj did everything slowly. "Christina," he would say reprovingly. He probably wouldn't stop her, and he probably wouldn't tell, because he wanted her to help him raise money for Disney World, but he certainly wouldn't hide out with her.

That left Jonah. But he was being poopy. Don't

fight, don't start things. Why share a hideaway with him?

She let her mind drift over Blake, pretending she could live here with him. Handsome, perfect Blake. Anya's boyfriend, however. Anya's rescuer, too. Blake had taken Anya away from the Shevvingtons, stashing her with some relative of his in the city while he finished up at boarding school.

The winter before, Christina had had such a crush on Blake! The crush had left her panting and trembling, dizzy and excited. Blake, of course, had not noticed. Eighteen-year-olds did not pay attention to the emotions of thirteen-year-olds. But Christina knew how love felt now, and Jonah did not inspire love. Jonah was just Jonah.

She sighed. Blake would be too busy driving his sports car and dressing in his catalog Maine clothing to bother with games in a storm cottage.

Christina checked the kitchen drawer. (There was only one drawer in the whole cottage.) Cheap forks, knives, and spoons; a spatula, a steak knife, can opener, and screwdriver. On a shelf were dented pots, ancient plastic plates, and a lemonade pitcher. Christina peeked under the sink. One squirt of dish soap, one stained sponge, and a box of kitchen matches.

I could have a cookout, thought Christina. No. People would see the smoke and investigate. Besides, then Benji would be right. It's one thing to creep in and out. It's another thing entirely to cook a hamburger in the fireplace.

Christina set the kitchen table for one and pretended to have pancakes, bacon, orange juice, and grapefruit halves with extra spoonfuls of sugar. I'm thirteen and playing house, she thought. This is so silly. In seventh grade, you're supposed to grow up, not down.

She put everything away exactly as she had found it.

Her bad moods never lasted long and this one was gone. Pleased with her hideaway, Christina decided to go make friends with the seventh grade again. She slid out the window, tucked the shutter in, and ran back down the cliffs.

Far away, in the cupola of Schooner Inne, sun glinted off a pair of binoculars.

Chapter 6

"This," said Robbie to Mr. O'Neil, the social worker, "is my cousin."

Christina tried to look like an Armstrong cousin. She had had a bad day in school and was rather hoping the afternoon trip to the mental institution would be a nice ride.

"Her name is Iris," added Robbie.

Iris? Christina wished she could have chosen her own fake name. If I could pick, she thought, it would be a name soft and beautiful. Now she was stuck with Iris. Still, it was fun to be a different person for an afternoon. Christina filled her head with Iris-type thoughts.

The social worker was big but limp. Shaking hands with him was like holding a wet sneaker. Mr. O'Neill drove slumped over the steering wheel and talked slow; even his cheeks drooped. How could a visit from this lump cheer anybody up?

He also asked too many questions. Christina knew nothing about Robbie's family. What was she supposed to say when he asked was Iris related by blood to the Armstrongs?

"No," said Robbie, "she's on my mother's side. She's a Murch."

Iris Murch? thought Christina. I can't stand this.

The social worker said, "Robbie, next time you might want to drive up with the Shevvingtons. They visit your sister every week. They're such fine people. Why, Val is practically catatonic; she hardly ever speaks; she's almost unreachable. Yet week after week Mr. and Mrs. Shevvington are there to encourage and comfort." He shook his big, loose head, like a cow shaking away flies. "What fine people," he repeated.

Week after week . . . the Shevvingtons appearing by Val's bed . . . creeping up like rodents in the dark . . . smiling in front of the staff, and gloating when they were alone with Val.

Christina imagined Mrs. Shevvington rocking with silent laughter, looking down at Val. Val, huddled under the pitiful protection of a hospital blanket, hiding from the very people who had put her in that prison. Of course Val will never get well, thought Christina. Not when the Shevvingtons come every week to renew her terror.

"They'll be so glad Val's cousin is visiting," added the social worker. "They'll want to meet you, Iris. Where do you go to school, anyway?"

Robbie said quickly, "Her parents teach her at home. You've heard of that. Home schooling. They don't approve of public schools. Or private schools, either."

The social worker said, "How fascinating, Iris. I would love to discuss that with your parents. Are they in town, too?"

"No," said Christina firmly. "Where is this hospital, anyway? Are we almost there? Do you think we could turn on the radio?" She hissed in Robbie's ear, "You dodo. What if he tells the Shevvingtons about me?"

Robbie said loudly, "Don't introduce Iris to the Shevvingtons. Her parents hate anybody that teaches school. They had very bad experiences when they were young. Her parents will never let Iris visit Val again if you mention school principals."

"What a fascinating neurosis," said Mr. O'Neill. "I promise, Iris. I can see you have a difficult life, and I don't want to add to it."

They traveled on, Christina making desperate meaningless conversation with Robbie about the baseball season. Nerves made Christina laugh as if she, too, were insane. The social worker watched in his rearview mirror, trying to identify *her* neurosis.

Suddenly, at a turn in the road, a high iron fence jumped up from the fields and flowers. Wire was woven among the black spikes, making the fence impassable from either side. A small white sign read "Shoreline Institute for the Mentally Troubled. Check in at gate. Visitors by pass only."

A guard stood in a little cubicle, swinging car gates open by pressing a button. He wrote down all their names. Iris Murch had just become real.

Mr. O'Neill said he would be visiting patients in another hall; Robbie and Iris could be with Val for half an hour, and then they were to wait for him in the Visitors' Lounge where, he assured them, a color television would keep them happy and occupied.

They parked.

Silent, empty cars glistened in the sun.

From the buildings came no sound; on the grass nobody walked. And yet there must be patients living behind each pane of glass.

They entered a wide lobby with polished floors and a smiling receptionist in a white uniform. "Doesn't it look like a Fat Farm," whispered Robbie, "where you pay a fortune to eat nothing and get massages?" But the hall doors were keyed; you could not get in or out without an attendant. The attendant on Val's hall was a man in white: white shirt, pants, socks, and shoes, as if he intended to blend in with the white walls and the white sheets. Christina worried about all these confused patients with no way to exit. "What do you do if there's a fire?" she said uneasily.

"Don't you think about that," said the attendant, patting her. "It's all arranged." He smiled at Christina. The teeth were Mrs. Shevvington's — wrinkled, dried corn on the cob. Christina shuddered. The attendant smiled even wider. Whispering, as if it were study hall, he breathed, "And what is your name?"

Patients' rooms stretched on either side, but there was no talk, no laughter, no radios, no yelling. If she looked in the rooms would they be like the guest rooms at Schooner Inne — occupied only by ghosts?

"My name is Iris," she whispered back.

In the first room, a man sat in a chair, looking at nothing, mouth hanging open, no sound coming out.

"They drug them," whispered Robbie. "That way the staff doesn't have to do anything."

Christina and Robbie walked slower, as if they too had been drugged and were sliding into a silent world.

"Here is your room," whispered the attendant. He took Christina's arm, as if he were about to lock her in. His hand was thick and inhuman, like a rubber glove filled with sand.

Robbie betrayed me! thought Christina, dizzy with shock. He and the Shevvingtons planned this. Robbie is going to have me admitted as Iris Murch. Nobody will ever see Christina Romney again. The attendant and the social worker are part of it. They didn't need eighteen days! They just needed one afternoon. And Robbie.

Christina tried to free herself but the attendant's grip had hardened like cement. She swung fear-wide eyes toward Robbie, but he was staring at his shoes. The attendant's lips never covered his yellow teeth. His smile stayed on and on, like a frozen frame in a movie.

If I can break free, she thought, I can run down the hall. But I have no key to let myself out. A patient's window? No. The glass is lined with wire. Even if I got into the yard, the fence has no toeholds. There's no way over.

She had a vision of her future: white walls, television with the sound turned off, attendants with triumphant smiles.

"Chrissie, relax," muttered Robbie. "It's not that bad. Val just lies there. What's the matter? You look as if you're having a breakdown yourself."

He had called her Chrissie, not Iris. She whirled. The attendant was back at the other end of the hall, keying himself out.

I fell into paranoia, thought Christina. I thought *They* were after me, all of *Them*. I thought *They* had a conspiracy against me.

How easy it was, then, to go crazy. All you had to do was think about it, and you began to fall toward it, the tilting floor of your own mind sliding you into a crack that would smash shut.

Val was exceptionally pretty.

Christina had expected someone beaten and bruised. Someone on whom the Shevvingtons' handiwork would show.

But the girl sitting cross-legged in the center of the neatly made bed had big brown eyes, tan skin, long lashes, and a wide firm mouth. She wore khaki pants and a cotton sweater, white with horizontal khaki stripes. Val looked like a girl who danced and partied; whose laughter was a shout of glee.

But Val did not blink. Her huge eyes just sat there. When Robbie and Christina crossed the room, the eyes did not follow them. The eyes did not see; needed no tears. Mrs. Shevvington's eyes, thought Christina. That's how the Shevvingtons got inside her. Through the eyes.

Robbie sat beside his sister, and the bed sank down, making her slender body tip against him. "Val?" he said. "I've brought you a friend. Her name is — " Robbie stopped, not knowing which name to use.

"I'm Anya's friend, from Burning Fog Isle," said Christina softly. "Do you remember Anya? You two used to be in school together."

Val got lower and lower in the bed, as if assuming a fetal position. She spoke in a voice so light it felt like a draft. *"Anya!"* Like air escaping from a balloon. *"Anya is next."*

"No. Anya is safe. Anya got away."

There was a conversation between them, one which Robbie was not part of. Val's eyes cleared, and she made her first blink. It took a great effort, as if her lids scraped and ached. *"Anya is safe?"*

"Anya is safe," said Christina firmly. "I saved her. Now she's living in the city with friends. She won't be back for a long time."

"I won't be back for a long time, either," whispered Val.

"Come back," said Christina urgently. "I need

55

you. Come back now, Val. Because *I'm* next."

Val's eyes opened even wider. She seemed to suck Christina in through her pupils. She leaned toward Christina. Her fingers grappled with Christina's dangling hair, gathering it in her hands like a harvest. "Then what are you doing here? The Shevvingtons might come!" She never raised her voice. As if the Shevvingtons' ears were pressed to cracks.

"I live with them," said Christina. "I have to board at Schooner Inne. Like Anya."

"They'll get you," said Val. Suddenly her voice was normal. As if having the Shevvingtons win were also normal.

Christina shook her head. "No, they won't. I know their plan."

"It doesn't help to know their plan. They get the other adults on their side. They get your parents and your teachers. They get psychiatrists. They make up lies. They corner you. They crowd you."

Val's huge eyes stared into a white corner of her white room, as if seeing a white rat there, trapped, caught, destroyed.

"If you're next, and you know it," whispered Val, "you must run." She lay back on her bed. Suddenly she was limp as a wet dishrag. Just clothes lying on the bedcovers, with no body inside them.

"Come back!" said Christina authoritatively.

But Val did not come back.

Robbie talked.

Christina talked.

But Val was not there. She was gone. Lost perhaps in her own head. Or floating in the room.

Or perhaps her soul lived in Number 7 at Schooner Inne. Only her flesh was in this institution. Attendants dressed an empty body in this cotton sweater and khaki pants. Val was trapped forever in a room of crimson and blue that stared into the tides of the mind.

"Half hour's up," said the attendant cheerily. He looked pleased to see Val lying on the bed like a dead person. "She's always like that," he confided. "We prop her up to take food."

Christina's hair separated with horror: the silver and gold standing apart from the brown. The attendant said, "What interesting hair," and without asking he touched it. She leaped away from him, into the hall.

Val's doe eyes fixed on the white corner and the white floor.

"Let's watch TV in the lounge," said Robbie. The attendant keyed them into the lounge. What a slick, shiny room it was. All its furniture could be scrubbed. There was no personality in it, as if mops and detergents had been used to scour away any trace of humankind. The television was twice the size of most, and the people in the soap opera more life-size than the silent patients in their rooms.

Robbie hissed, "Lie down. Roll over. Hide."

"What am I, a hound dog?" said Christina.

Robbie kicked her. "The Shevvingtons are here!" he hissed.

Christina lay down, rolled over, and tried to hide behind a couch. But this was not a place where hiding was allowed. No drapes hung to the floor, no skirts surrounded chairs, no doors jutted out. In the corners of the room, video cameras scanned for missing patients.

Robbie ran to the door of the lounge to keep the Shevvingtons from coming in. "Hi, Mrs. Shevvington," he called out. "I just visited Val. She's the same as ever. How are you?"

"My goodness, Robbie, you're in a lively mood today," said Mrs. Shevvington. "I suppose it's the thought of finishing seventh grade up in only a few days, isn't it?" She laughed merrily. No doubt for the benefit of other people listening: a psychiatrist or parents.

I am in a mental institution hiding behind a see-through couch, pretending to be Iris Murch, thought Christina. This really is lunatic. If they see me . . .

Even underneath the couch was clean. This place was remarkable. Somebody must mop upside down.

The social worker's floppy voice said, "Well, Robbie, where's your cousin? We need to be leaving."

"Cousin?" repeated Mrs. Shevvington. Her voice folded around him like a blanket. "Why, Robbie, who is that? I don't recall meeting any of your family except your parents."

Christina drew into a tuck, like Val, whimpering, praying not to be caught.

"I guess she's still with Val," said Robbie brightly. "Let's find her."

Three pairs of feet passed the lounge door. Mr. Shevvington's shoes were black and gleaming. Mrs. Shevvington's were red with heels like stabbing knives. Robbie had on dirty and torn sneakers. Christina's palm left a sweaty handprint on the linoleum.

In the front hall she heard Mr. O'Neill chatting with the receptionist. She got up and sauntered out, wondering who was watching the cameras and what they thought and what they would do. "Hi, Mr. O'Neill. I'll wait for you in the car," she said. He was too nerdy to sense anything strange.

Out in the sunshine, Christina nearly danced across the smooth golf-green grass. I'm free, I'm safe! But that might look crazed. So she walked sedately to the car.

Strewn over the backseat were matches. The tools of an arsonist. The joy of a child insane with the love of fire. "Poor little Christina," the Shevvingtons would say. "See how she crept into the mental home. A plea, of course. Crying out for help. Saying, lock me up before I set fire to something or hurt somebody! Poor little dear. So demented she can't even use her real name."

Christina gathered the matches desperately. There were so many she could hardly hold them in her cupped hands. Stooping, slithering, she rushed among the parked cars to the Shevvingtons' van.

It was locked.

She could not get rid of the matches.

They would find her — they knew they would — they were on their way. They would bring witnesses — it was just as Val had predicted — it didn't matter that she knew the plan. They would still win — she would be caught clutching the matches to her heart!

Val had known, Val had said *run*!

The car next to the Shevvingtons was unlocked. Christina ripped open the back door, threw the matches in, and shoveled them beneath the driver's seat.

Panting, she leaped back to the social worker's car, where she lay curled on the backseat, hidden from the windows and eyes of the Institute.

How did the Shevvingtons plan so easily?

What ally did the Shevvingtons have, that Christina did not know about? Was it Michael? Was it Benj? Was it Jonah?

Chapter 7

The air was hot and heavy and full of omens.

Not a leaf stirred. Not a hair on Christina's head lifted.

The air did not want to be breathed. When Christina filled her lungs, the air objected, lying thick inside her, making her cough.

"An electrical storm coming," said Jonah uneasily.

They were standing on the top of the cliffs. Rocks above them, rocks below them. The Atlantic was between tides and merely lapped at its boundaries instead of fighting or fleeing them. Seaweed lay like sickness on the surface.

The sky turned strange colors, as if becoming ill. Christina held her hands up to the heavens.

"Don't do that," said Jonah. "You look —"

He broke off. Christina turned to look at him, her eyes huge in her face, her separate colors of hair tangled above her head like —

"Snakes," said Jonah, shivering. "You look like

someone from a Greek myth, like some ancient woman spying on the gods on Olympus."

Christina laughed. But her laugh, too, was ancient, as if her mind and body had been scooped up by another time, another power.

Jonah tried to talk to her about school, about himself. Christina did not listen to him. She floated at the cliff edge. I'm ready to leave the world, she thought. Where would I be going if I went?

"We'd better go inside," said Jonah. His nervousness was as palpable as the coming storm. "If lightning strikes, it'll strike here. We're higher than anything."

She would not go. She could imagine herself, outlined against the bruised sky: the long wild skirt, the slender ankles below, the upstretched hands, and the tangled mane of hair. Christina wanted summer people and painters and photographers to see her and immortalize her. She wanted to be strange and different and weird.

"Come in!" cried Jonah.

The sky split open. A sheet of silver sliced into the sea like javelins thrown by angry gods.

Jonah grabbed her hand and yanked her toward the big green doors of Schooner Inne.

"I want to watch the lightning," whispered Christina. She could feel the electricity in her hair. The electricity came in her own three colors.

Jonah shoved her ahead of him.

"I want to *be* the lightning!" she cried.

He bundled her in the door. "We'll watch from

the window," he said, and the sky went crazy. Lightning, rain, and wind burst forth.

Jonah slammed the door behind them.

Christina pressed her palms against the door as if to embrace the weather.

Jonah said shakily, "Chrissie, you're too much for me. I think maybe when the storm's over, I'll just go on home."

She came down to earth in a hurry. She was just a seventh-grade girl with a boy she liked. "Don't go, Jonah. I'm sorry I went off with Robbie yesterday instead of you. And you're wrong to think there's something between Benj and me. Except Burning Fog. He's my brother."

Jonah kept furniture between them like a shield. "You made me think of Anya," he said. His voice shook. "Remember how she went crazy last winter? That's how you looked out there, trying to hold hands with the lightning."

"Oh, Jonah, I was not. Don't exaggerate. I just like weather. That's what it is to be an island girl. You're one with the weather."

"But you're not on the island now," he said.

"I am always on the island," said Christina. What made me say that? she wondered. It will scare him more. Why do I want to scare him? She made her eyes glitter to match her lightning-rod hair, and Jonah shivered, and went home.

She was alone in the sea captain's house, alone in the rooms furnished for the bride who flung herself to the rocks all those years ago. She felt the sea calling her name; felt the lightning clapping its hands — crying — *Christina . . . Christina. . . .*

The syllables of her name shivered through the house, like Jonah leaving. Like leaves falling. *Chhhhrisssss . . .* said the house.

"Shhh!" said Christina.

Chhhhrrissssss . . . said the house.

It was upstairs. She stood at the bottom of the steps, staring up into the dizzying circle of tipping white balconies. Gripping the banister she went up, step by step. "Who's calling me?" she said loudly.

The carpet muffled her steps.

The emptiness in the house smothered her heartbeat.

Chhhhrrisssss . . . said the house.

Above her the floor creaked.

"Who's there?" cried Christina Romney.

Beyond the cupola windows, lightning lit the sky. Thunder crashed. The tide began to change, and the ocean began to sing. From everywhere, from nowhere, the world whispered, *Chhhhrrisssss. . . .*

She stood on the second floor.

She ripped open the door to Anya's room, that room of silver and gray, of fragile lace and airspun gauze.

It was gone.

The room was on fire.

Curls of flame and gleaming angry coals cried her name.

It became my room, thought Christina. I knew

it would happen. Val knew it would happen. They have me. A room of fire and islands. I was falling into this room even while Jonah was standing there. I'll never get out. This is the other world I knew was waiting for me.

Christina . . . said the voice beyond the walls, behind the fires . . . *Christina* . . . *stay here.* . . .

If I can get out of the room, thought Christina, if I can take a step backward, I can save myself.

She tried to breathe, but the air in the house was as thick and smothery as the air outside. She turned. She fell. She crawled toward the stairs, toward the opening — any opening — anything at all. The banisters were white prison bars, the stairway descended . . . but the voice stayed upstairs.

"Dialing the emergency number?" said Mrs. Shevvington, in a voice as thick as mud. Her heavy hands closed on Christina's thin shoulders and moved her away from the telephone.

"Fire," mumbled Christina. "There's a fire upstairs."

"Is there?" Mrs. Shevvington's smile was a crack in the cold, congealed oatmeal of her face. "A fire that you set, Christina? We have your fingerprints, you know," she said very softly. "On that tin can you put that candle in." Her voice was air, without form and texture. "The one you like to light in your bedroom." The voice crawled on Christina's skin.

"The one you took downstairs, and tried to hide behind the geraniums."

The house had turned silent. No voices anywhere.

Mr. Shevvington stood behind his wife, stiff as a mannequin, his fine tailored suit just hanging there, as if he had stepped out for a while, leaving his flesh behind. His eyes glowed like coals of blue ice.

The hottest fires are blue, not yellow. He's going to set fire to me, she thought.

"What a wharf rat you are, Christina," remarked Mrs. Shevvington. "Good for nothing. Destructive behavior whenever you think nobody is looking."

"There is no fire," said Mr. Shevvington, and his voice laughed like a little brook in the spring, tumbling over smooth rocks. "Come, Christina. Let's look."

He dragged her up the stairs. He said, "You've been complaining about your little attic room, Christina. You've been telling the children at school that criminals have better housing than you do. If only you had confided in us — why, we would have moved you immediately. But we're moving you now, Christina."

He propelled her into room number 8. She tried to get free. He was as strong as Michael. She could not twist loose. She was the kitten, on her way to the vet's, to be put down.

Where are the boys? thought Christina. Why aren't they home yet? I need them. I need Benj.

"Michael and Benjamin are both staying at friends' houses for the night," said Mrs. Shevvington. "What a shame that you have no friends, Christina. Nobody ever asks you to spend the night."

She was in Room 8. They were blocking the doorway. She was trapped. Mrs. Shevvington's thick body and Mr. Shevvington's striped suit filled the only exit.

Chhhhrisssstina . . . said the voice beyond the walls. *Chhhhrisssstina* . . . it cried from behind the fires . . . *stay here* . . .

"A cold fire?" she said, confused. She stretched out her hands to warm them in front of the flickering flames. But the fire stayed cold and metallic. Behind it was a wall of foggy sea, painted with seawater itself, and a suggestion of an island: a mere whiff of island. Seagulls and twisted pines beckoned. *Chhhhrisssstina* . . . said the voice beyond the walls. *Chhhhrisssstina* . . . *stay here* . . .

"Home," whispered Mrs. Shevvington. "This is home."

"Home," repeated Christina. "This is home."

Mrs. Shevvington sat on the pretty bed, sinking in the soft mattress. She took Christina in her lap, as so often she had held Dolly. "It's nice to be home at last, isn't it, Christina, darling?"

Christina nodded.

"You'll sleep well here, won't you Christina, dear?"

Christina nodded.

"Among the fire and islands," said Mrs. Shevvington, like a lullaby. "The sea keeps count, you know. It wants one of you."

"Me," said Christina. "It can have me."

Mrs. Shevvington rocked her and rocked her. "It will," said Mrs. Shevvington. "It will."

Chapter 8

In the night, the sea tried to crumble the foundation of the house.

Down in the cove, down among the rocks, the sea fingered every crevice, washed into every crack. The tide rose, and the sea shouldered its way into the cliff, calling, *Chhhrrrrrissssssteeeennnaaahh.*

She heard it break into the house, she heard it filling the cellar, she heard it lapping up the stairs, calling her name.

A foghorn blew deep and throbbingly out at sea.

Half of her woke up and half of her slid between cracks, like the sea. She did not know where she was. In a boat? On Burning Fog Isle? In her attic bedroom?

She sat up. The room around her slowly came into dark, nightlike focus. It was guest room number 8. She was alone in the house with the voices and the sea and the Shevvingtons.

Wake up all the way, she ordered herself. Or else you'll wake in the morning and be part of the room

. . . like the girls before you. The room and the Shevvingtons will own you. Like Val in the mental hospital, you'll be a body for strangers to dress, drug, and prop in front of a television . . . while you, Christina, drift on a painted sea to a fiery isle. . . .

She dragged herself out of the drug of fear.

Had it been easier for Val to let herself sift like flour into insanity? Had Val tired of fighting, she thought, just as you have tired of keeping your eyes open?

She had never slept on the second floor before. The house creaked differently; the ocean was louder. But oh, so distinct! So clear! A voice like a solo in a concert.

Chhhrrrrissssssteeennnaaahh . . . sang the ocean.

The creak, like the sea, came nearer.

The creak gathered rhythm, and volume, and creaked on into guest room number 8.

The door moved.

No, she told herself. It didn't move. It was open like that before, wasn't it?

She could actually hear the water in the house. The ocean had come for her. Just as Anya had foretold. *The sea, Chrissie, the sea wants one of us.* And last night Christina had promised Mrs. Shevvington — it can have me, Mrs. Shevvington!

Something moved behind the door.

Something that breathed and waited and reached.

She could not look; not even she, Christina, granite of the Isle. She closed her eyes while her lungs jerked for air and her skin shivered with fear.

And into the soft fog of the room came the ocean, crying, *Chhhrrrrisssssssteeennnaaahh*; crying, *here I am, move over, I've come for you.*

It came swaying. Crawling.

Christina whimpered, and the tears flowed down her cheeks, and she thought: Tears are saltwater; soon I will be all tears — all saltwater — vanished into the ocean.

It got into the bed with her.

Its fingers closed around her skin.

Christina's scream of horror pierced the silent night. It cut through the plaster walls and through the cracks of doors and through the white forest of tilting rails on tilting balconies.

The hand of the ocean covered Christina's mouth and the ocean murmured, "It's just me. Val. I ran away from the Institute. I've been hiding in the room next door. I've been calling your name all night, Christina, so you'd come and find me. Instead you've gone and screamed, and now the Shevvingtons will come in to see what is the matter and they'll know I'm here."

Christina was as flat as one of the sheets on her bed. She thought she would probably never speak again, or think, or stand up. Val added proudly, "I've been so clever. I got out of the Institute, and nobody saw me. Even with all their cameras and bed checks and supervisors, nobody saw."

Christina waited for her scream to bring the Shevvingtons.

But it did not.

She knew they had heard the scream. People in Utah had probably heard the scream. Her hair was damp from the sweat of terror and the pillow damp from the tears of fear. Why had the Shevvingtons not come running?

And then she remembered. These were the Shevvingtons. She was always expecting them to be like regular grown-ups, even after all this time. To protect and to worry. But they never protected. Never worried. No. The Shevvingtons planned and gloated instead.

"Don't worry," she said to Val. "They want me to be afraid. They are probably awake and happy because of that scream." She thought of their smiles: Mr. Shevvington's, smooth and hidden in the dark; Mrs. Shevvington's, yellow and curled at his side.

And I, she thought, am no longer half here. I am all here. "Thank you, Val," she whispered, hugging the other girl. "I nearly slipped into the crack. You saved me."

She turned on the tiny lamp by the bedside table.

In the half light, fire and smoke seemed to creep out of the cracks of the walls. For a moment she was ready to run, ready to scream *Fire!*, to save Val as she had once saved Dolly.

It's just paint, she thought. Anya fell into the changing posters of the sea that Mrs. Shevvington put in her room. I will fall into the mural they've painted on the wall. This afternoon I panicked. I was expecting fire so it became fire.

I must remember that. Things become what you expect them to become. But I am granite. Nothing can shatter me.

Christina lay back on the pillow again, comforted.

"Now hide me somewhere," whispered Val.

"Why can't you go home? I haven't met your mother and father, but Robbie is nice. Just explain that you're better and you can live at home now."

"You don't understand. They think the Shevvingtons know best. The Institute has probably already telephoned them. And all they would do is call an ambulance and send me back."

A year ago, Christina would never have believed that. Now she believed.

"I can't hide here, either." Val's voice was breath, without tone. "The Shevvingtons chose the Institute. They'd love driving me back there. Shutting the gates. Closing the glass. Smiling sadly when I tried to explain."

The house creaked.

Val whimpered.

Even when there are no footsteps, thought Christina, in this house you hear them. You hear the ghosts of these rooms, all the souls trying to get free of the Shevvingtons.

Outside the ocean spit water against the cliffs, but it did not call her name. Had it been Val whispering *Christina*? Or the ocean? And why wasn't it talking now? Was the ocean just resting between tides?

Between victims?

In the morning, thought Christina, I will go to the hardware store and buy a gallon of paint. I will paint over these walls. I will paint away the fire and the fog. I will say to the Shevvingtons, "It's my room and I like it plain white." With a paintbrush I will end the nightmare.

She imagined herself flicking paint in their eyes if they argued.

She imagined them taking the tin can with the candle and the fingerprints to the police, and telling them of arson; imagined the ambulance coming for her as well as for Val. Imagined the Shevvingtons saying to her mother and father, You tried — but sometimes mental illness seizes a child no matter how well intentioned the parents; nobody knows better than we; are we not suffering the very same catastrophe that you are? Our only son locked up just as your only daughter must be? Be brave, like us, and say good-bye to the Christina you once knew.

"The storm cottage," breathed Christina. "Val, that's where you can hide! Nobody will look there. The summer people don't come till August." Christina slid out of the bed. She pulled on jeans and yanked her sweatshirt over her head.

"Step where I step," instructed Christina in the softest voice she had. "Skip stairs where I skip."

Val said, "Shouldn't we wait till the sun comes up?"

Christina shook her head. "People might see us," she whispered.

Down, down they went: ghosts on the run.

As they went lower and lower, Christina smelled the tide. For a moment she could not take the last step off the stairs, for fear she would tumble into the sea. It was right here — right in the house!

Val said, "The cellar is full of water. I know because I tried to hide there. It chased me up the stairs."

The snick of the front door lock seemed loud as a cannon. They waited, but the Shevvingtons' bedroom door did not open.

They slid out, and eased the door shut behind them.

The stars in the sky trembled.

The waves in the ocean fluttered.

They scuttled over rocks and sand, past deserted docks, and silent parked cars.

"I know what happened," said Christina, disgusted with herself. Why, oh, why did she let herself yarn? Michael was right; Christina would stretch any story at all. The cannon strength of the tides had broken through the cellar passage, that was all. It was open again. The flimsy cement layer the Shevvingtons had used to block up their son's creepy entrance had burst.

"Honestly," said Christina to Val, "I'm such a

dodo bird. I make such a big deal out of every little thing."

The horizon glowed pink. The sun edged toward Maine. They had barely gotten past the wharf when the first lobsterman pulled up in his truck, stomped down the dock, started the engine on his boat.

Silent as seabirds they crept around the closed cottages.

"This is perfect," said Christina happily. "You'll be safe here, Val. Nobody can find you here."

In a window high in Schooner Inne, the first ray of sun glinted off a pair of binoculars.

Chapter 9

Christina had always wanted to stay up all night. Every time on Burning Fog Isle when she had a friend spending the night, she begged her parents to let them stay up all night, and her parents always said no.

But it was not as much fun as she had expected.

In school the next day, she was dizzy with sleepiness; her eyelids closed relentlessly. When her brain dredged for information, it found only grit.

She worried continually about Val, sleeping on bare metal springs in a vacant house. Was Val stable enough, well enough for such a night? Was it even safe for anybody to stay alone like that? Should Christina call Mr. and Mrs. Armstrong and tell them? Should Christina tell Robbie? Or Benj? Or her own mother and father?

But the Shevvingtons must have an ally she had not identified. What if the ally was Robbie? And when she said, "I have Val!" what if his mouth went thin and evil like Mrs. Shevvington's . . . his eyes hot and yellow like theirs?

As for Benj, last night when she could have used his granite, he had been elsewhere. At some meeting for Band, working on fund-raisers. Oh, sure, he said he wanted her help, but when push came to shove, he got all stuttery and embarrassed and said he couldn't bring a seventh-grader to the meeting. "I mean, girls like Astrid and Megan are going to be on the committee," he said helplessly. Astrid and Megan were impressive, exciting seniors. Once they had been best friends with Anya. But when Anya began to collapse, Astrid and Megan vanished. They weren't going to hang around with a failure. Christina would just as soon kick Astrid and Megan in the shins as work with them. "That's why you can't come," Benj had said at last. "You act like a seventh-grader, too."

I do not act like a seventh-grader! thought Christina resentfully, walking down middle school halls, passing middle school classrooms. Who saved Val, anyway?

But oh, how Christina wanted to lean on somebody. How she wanted a partner! Or at least some advice.

From some unknown source Val had acquired a surge of strength. But breaking out of the Institute, hitchhiking to the village, creeping into Schooner Inne, hiding from the Shevvingtons . . . all Val's resources were used up.

Now Val expected Christina to accomplish everything else — bring food and news and company. Find a way to make her freedom last. Save Val from going back. Prove that Val was well again. Prove, in fact, that she had never been ill to start with. That it was all the Shevvingtons' contrivance.

Christina did not have the slightest idea how to do any of that.

If only she had gotten a full night's rest. Then perhaps she could think clearly. As it was, all her thoughts were blurred.

In school it was Safety Week. Christina tried to open her eyes and concentrate on Safety. The Fire Department gave an assembly talk about safety with matches, lawnmowers, and barbecues.

Nobody in seventh grade wanted to be safe. What was exciting about safety? Everybody wanted to be in danger. In history they talked about terrorism and how it was sweeping the world. Jonah said, "I like terrorism. It's exciting to get on a plane and wonder if you'll be hijacked and end up a prisoner." Everybody agreed that was much more exciting than getting salted nuts for a snack.

In Art they had to make posters about safety, and in English Mrs. Shevvington made them write slogans for the posters. Christina was too tired even to hang onto a crayon, let along design something. "We're too old for this," she complained. "Elementary school kids have to make posters, but seventh-graders have outgrown it."

"Outgrown safety?" said Mrs. Shevvington. "How interesting, Christina. I shall bear that in mind."

"Yeah," said Gretch, "you should see what she's doing in woodworking. She's making a fire."

Mrs. Shevvington's little eyes flared. She turned her whole body, like a vehicle, and her flat oatmeal face fastened on Christina. "Making fires?" she repeated.

"We're all making summer fires," said Christina.

"But only yours," smirked Vicki, "has flames."

For Father's Day, the seventh-graders were painting plywood cut-outs to be placed in the empty fireplace for decoration during the summer. Most kids were doing geraniums or cats. Christina, however, thought a summer fire should be a fire, and hers was bigger than anybody's, with curling flames she had cut on the jigsaw. She had chosen metallic paint — bronze and gold with flecks that glittered.

"Oh, you know her fire obsession, Mrs. Shevvington," said Gretch. "You were the one who told us about it. Remember how she wrote essays over the winter about fire? About how she'd like to burn all her sweaters because she was so sick of them? Well, you should see how much she loves Woodworking. She can play with fire all — "

Christina was too tired to think. "You shut up!" she yelled. "Or I'll burn *you*!"

The room went silent.

The hum of fans and the whir of traffic invaded the room, like crawling insects. The eyes of the classroom rotated and fixed on Christina. Her threat seemed to hang in the room like loops of crepe paper, flaming, touching Gretchen.

Christina lifted her hands as if she could cut off the rays of their stares with her flat palms. Her lids scraped mercilessly over her dried-out eyes. Being so sleepy made her nervous and twitchy.

Am I really twitching? thought Christina. Is my cheek jerking like Robbie's? Are my hands knotting? Do I look insane? Or is it just inside my head where the twitching and the panting is going on?

"Christina," said Mrs. Shevvington. Her voice was silken now, drawing across Christina's cheek like a veil. "How queer you sound, my dear. First you don't care about Safety." Her voice curled like smoke and the room seemed to fog up.

Like the wall in bedroom number 8, Christina thought. I meant to buy paint today. Paint over the fire and islands. But instead I have to get food for Val.

"Then, Christina, dear, you tell us that only little children should worry about Safety?" The voice crept like a cat, playing with that word *safety*, mocking it, tossing it around like a dead mouse.

"Then you play with fire," whispered Mrs. Shevvington, her voice a wind that flickered flames. The classroom shivered. Even Jonah shivered. "And finally, Christina . . ." She spoke like the sea. *Chhhhrrissssteeenah*, she hissed. ". . . you threaten your classmates?"

Christina tried to wake up. She was falling into

a trap; she knew it, she could see the steel teeth of the jaws of the trap, but she could not run.

"*Chhhhrrissssteeenah!*" said Mrs. Shevvington, wet like tides, "what is that I see on your desk?"

The mass of eyes swerved and followed the thick, stubby, pointing finger. In her morning stupor, Christina had forgotten to bring her books to school, so the desktop was empty: just a rectangle of blonde wood with a groove for a pencil. Christina lowered her head, although she was so tired she was afraid she would drop down onto the desk and sleep: through school, or through life.

The desk was not empty.

Lying on the edge was a tiny box of matches, the kind with a little drawer, that Christina had used for bureaus for her dolls' bedrooms when she had had a dollhouse. The red tip of a single match stuck out of the tiny drawer.

Mrs. Shevvington gasped, and clutched her chest.

The seventh grade gasped, and covered their mouths.

"Yesterday on the playing field, matchbooks fell out of her jacket pocket," said Vicki.

"It's not mine," said Christina. She pushed the matchbox away, and it fell on the floor. The mass of eyes tilted to see the floor. She was no longer in a room with twenty-five thirteen-year-olds; they were just eyes. Eyes that peeked and peered.

"Stop staring at me!" Christina cried out.

The eyes turned away, full of pity, saying in eye

language, *poor Christina . . . poor Christina . . . poor sick Christina.*

Mrs. Shevvington knelt beside Christina's desk. Her oatmeal face was close to Christina's; her tiny yellow teeth near enough to bite. Her hand was so fat, the flesh grew over her rings, and her thick, bitten nails pressed jaggedy half moons into Christina's kneecap. Christina nearly gagged.

"You feel sick, don't you, Christina? What kind of sickness is it, Christina? Sickness of the heart? Or — sickness of the mind, my dear?" Her voice oozed like a jellyfish.

"It's sickness from cafeteria food," said Jonah loudly. "They served last week's tunafish."

"I had that," said Katy. "It was disgusting. I practically threw up."

Jonah and Katy batted words back and forth, like a ball over a volley net, and the eyes stopped staring, and Mrs. Shevvington stopped kneeling, and finally, finally, class was over.

Christina felt as fragile as spun glass. If somebody pushes me, she thought, I'll shatter.

Walking down the halls with the others, she tried to make herself small and safe. *What if a fire starts? They'll say that I —*

Somebody touched her. Christina leaped as if attacked by a nest of wasps. Gretch and Vicki snickered. "It's only your old lobsterman," they said.

It was Benj. She could not imagine what he was doing in this hallway. High school did not share corridors with middle school. Benj seemed out of breath, almost frantic. Had the Shevvingtons hurt Benj, too? I should be an owl, she thought, so I can swivel my head in all directions. I can't keep track of the Shevvingtons.

"You were in bed when I got home from our meeting," Benj said, "so I didn't get to tell you about it. The fund-raising committee," he added, because she looked so blank, "for Disney World. And guess what?" His eyes were fever-bright.

I have to feed Val, she thought, and paint the wall, and stay awake, and keep away from matches. "What?" she said dimly.

His voice was still as the surface of a pond. "I'm chairman," Benj told her.

School did not interest Benj and had little to do with his life. He had never joined anything except Band, never played a sport, never attended a show. It was Michael for whom the games and activities of school were lifeblood. For Benj only the sea mattered; only Burning Fog Isle, and his own boat.

Something in Christina awoke. Off to the side of her own problems, she remembered his. "You're chairman," Christina repeated. "Benj!" She hugged him. "I'm so proud of you."

He let out the puff of air he had been holding onto, and he grinned. "I've never done anything like this before, Chrissie," he confided. "I don't really know where to start. But I told everybody your ideas. The walk-a-thon. Car washes. Bake sales. But mostly the chowder-thon. Everybody said it was the best idea they'd ever heard. Even Astrid and Megan thought it was the best idea they'd ever heard. And they nominated *me* chairman!"

Vicki and Gretch snickered. Vicki said, "They just couldn't find a sucker to do it except you, Benjamin."

Christina backed up and jammed her shoe heel down toward the bare toes peeking out of Vicki's sandals.

"You missed," said Vicki sweetly.

Mrs. Shevvington caught up to them. "Why, Benjamin," she said, "what are you doing in the middle school wing? You know we can't have older, wilder boys around the younger children."

Vicki and Gretch giggled. "Older and wilder?" repeated Gretch scornfully, stroking her seal-smooth brown hair.

Mrs. Shevvington laughed a civilized little laugh. "Of course, you're right, girls. How silly of me. Benjamin may be older, but he's too dull to be wild. He couldn't corrupt a clam."

Threats filled Christina's head: terrible things to say and do to Mrs. Shevvington and Vicki and Gretch. I hate them! she thought. They can flatten anybody. All they need is bad words and good timing.

But Benjamin Jaye surprised her. He hardly heard Mrs. Shevvington. He certainly hadn't heard Vicki and Gretch; those two girls meant nothing to him; never had; never would.

Benj took Christina's waist in his two big work-man's hands and lifted her into the air. He swung her in a circle the way he would have swung his baby sister Dolly.

It was sheer athletic exuberence. Benjamin was overflowing with pride in himself: For the first time ever, he was stretching himself — doing more — reaching out — getting ready to pull something off: something that mattered.

Christina laughed, sharing his joy.

When he set her down she hugged him a second time and looked up into his face to admire his happiness. He looked down to share it with her and the world changed.

The halls vanished.

Mrs. Shevvington evaporated.

Vicki and Gretch were silent wraiths.

Jonah and Robbie were gone as if they had never been.

Benjamin's hands left her waist and found her hair. He separated the silver from the gold, the gold from the chocolate brown. He twined his fingers in her strange mass of tangled hair and tangled it more. He bent forward. His lips touched her forehead and seemed to hover there, as if all their lives had been waiting for this moment: waiting to be together.

Benj said, "The sophomore dance is Friday night." His voice was husky and muffled.

Christina thought, He has never asked anybody to go to a dance. He has never even thought of asking anybody to go to a dance.

"Will you go with me?" said Benj.

Chapter 10

"Christina," breathed Katy, awestruck and proud to be Christina's friend. Her plump cheeks grew even fatter with her excited smile. "You're going to the *sophomore* dance? With Benjamin Jaye? The one whose muscles split open the sleeves of his T-shirts?"

Christina paraded in front of the seventh-grade girls. I am the only one, she thought, going to a high school dance. Even Vicki and Gretch are no-bodies compared to me. Christina's head sang songs of triumph. Her feet danced rhythms of conquering.

"He's just a smelly old lobsterman," said Vicki contemptuously. "Who would want to go anywhere with Old Benj?"

"Besides," said Gretch, giggling, "it's not a real date. Christina's practically his sister. Everybody's related to everybody on that silly island. A *real* date would be Benjamin asking a *real* person. Somebody from the mainland."

"But who from the mainland would go anywhere

with that dim old fisherman?" snickered Vicki.

"Here's what their conversation will be," said Gretch. "Christina will babble about fires and islands. Benj will grunt. Christina will babble about safety posters and woodworking class. Benj will grunt." Gretch and Vicki grunted at each other, laughing hysterically.

"Don't hit them," said Jonah in an undertone. "Chrissie, get a grip on yourself. Mrs. Shevvington is watching. Don't hit Vicki or Gretch."

"Hit them?" said Christina gaily. "I hardly even hear them. They're just little seventh-graders. I'm the one going to a high school dance." She began dancing with Jonah, gripping his hand, swinging him back, yanking herself in, taking up the entire hall in her exuberance.

Jonah let her dance him like a puppet. Then he said hesitantly, "But they're right, aren't they? You are just going as island friends, aren't you?"

Christina could feel the separate colors of her hair dazzling in the sun's rays. She felt herself giving off heat — sparkling from behind her eyes. She danced away from Jonah, off by herself, wearing the gown of her golden hair. I am on fire, she thought. I might even decide to fall in love.

The seventh-graders stared after her. The girls were half envious and half afraid. They could not imagine going anywhere with a real live sixteen-year-old boy.

Vicki whispered, "You know what I bet?"

"What?" said the seventh-grade girls. They wondered how did Christina suddenly get so much older than they were? What did Christina have to offer that they did not?

"I bet Christina's going to be a wharf rat."

"No, she won't," said Jonah.

"You always defend her," said Gretch. "Your opinion doesn't count."

Jonah wanted to run after Christina and warn her, but he didn't want to be teased by Vicki and Gretch. He hated being teased. Hated the way Vicki and Gretch could flick words around like the tip of a whip.

Nor could he stay among these girls any longer. Like some great ugly hen, Mrs. Shevvington was spreading her filthy wings over her brood. The girls were clucking like her; scratching in the dirt like her. Jonah felt as if any moment the girls would start pecking Christina. They wanted to say vicious things; he could feel their eagerness to repeat anything Mrs. Shevvington said.

"What is a wharf rat, anyway?" asked Katy.

"A girl," said Mrs. Shevvington, "who works in factories and has babies before she's sixteen."

Jonah fled.

"A girl who loses all her teeth and doesn't get false ones," said Vicki, loudly, so the words would follow Jonah and sink into his vision. "Like that girl who pumps gas at the town dock and eats ten jelly doughnuts at a time. She's only seventeen. That's a wharf rat."

Katy said desperately, "I don't think that would

happen to Christina. She has plans. She's going to amount to something." Down the hall Christina Romney danced alone, the ceiling lights turning her hair to spun gold, and then to threads of silver.

"What about Anya?" countered Gretchen. "She was supposed to graduate first in her class, and what happened? She dropped out of high school last winter to work at the laundromat. That was her big starry future. Folding other people's underwear."

"I am afraid," said Mrs. Shevvington sadly, "that all too often that's what happens to island girls. All they can do is work at the cannery, canning fish."

Vicki laughed. "Benj can catch 'em," she snickered. "Christina can can 'em."

"We can certainly hope Christina does not fall into the same grim future as those examples," said Mrs. Shevvington. "You girls must keep an eye on her."

All their eyes were on her. She was dancing back toward them now, and they had no idea what they would say to her, or think of her.

"That's what school is all about," said Mrs. Shevvington softly. "Forming a community to help one another. Poor Christina is in a time of trouble. This appalling obsession with fire is becoming quite an emotional problem."

Katy remembered the woman on the dock — only seventeen years old! Could that happen to small, slim, brave Christina? Mrs. Shevvington knew about these things. And Mrs. Shevvington said . . .

* * *

At lunch, although she was starving, Christina ate nothing. She took food from the cold line — a sandwich, a yogurt, an apple. Talking brightly to Jonah, she removed each piece of food to her lap, wrapped it into a napkin without looking, and slid it carefully into her bookbag. There, she thought proudly. Food for Val.

"Look out for the Shevvingtons," muttered Jonah. "I know you think you've seen everything they can do, but they're crafty. They're going to turn all the girls against you. You've got to pay attention, Chrissie."

Christina thought of all she had accomplished lately: getting into the Institute as Iris Murch, making friends with Val, smuggling Val into the storm cottage, and all the while telling Benj how to raise money, and having him fall in love with her. It was amazing how much strength you got just from knowing that a boy adored you. You could take on the world when a boy ached for you. The Shevvingtons. Hah! Small potatoes. Hardly worth a thought, let alone panic. "Jonah, I'm smarter."

Jonah's face curled: nose, lips, even cheeks, making a big, dumb, seventh-grade face. "Don't be so cocky."

"You're just jealous, Jonah, because I'm going out with Benjamin."

"Oh, it's going out now, is it? You're dating now, huh? Fine. Date him. See if I care." Jonah crumpled his brown lunch bag, threw it violently into a trash can, and stomped away.

In woodworking, Christina painted her summer fire.

"What color is fire anyway?" she muttered to herself. She struck a match and studied the flame, how it was yellow, blue, white. The flame from the match was not much to get excited about. "I want a fiercer fire," she told the teacher. She mixed scarlet and orange into her yellow, until the tips of the flames glittered savagely.

When she turned from admiring her work, Mr. Shevvington was standing behind her. "Christina?" he said. The word floated like a leaf, staying aloft. As concerned principal, Mr. Shevvington talked with the woodworking teacher about poor Christina — about how the administration was worried. Was Christina, perhaps, a bit unnatural in her interest in fire? A bit . . . not to exaggerate . . . but . . . a bit *dangerous*?

Christina set her summer fire against the wall to dry. He didn't scare her. She was full of philosophy and love. She was protected by the colors of her hair, by Benj's crush, by her own isle, far out at sea, waiting for her to come home.

Mr. Shevvington's big sad eyes caught the eyes of the class. He tilted his elegant head to the side, pitying Christina. The class, like sunflowers worshiping, tilted with him, growing sad, full of pity.

Mr. Shevvington shook his head slowly. Once.

The class shook its head slowly. Once. Like a decision: a decree.

She's crazy. She's not one of us. Keep your eyes on her.

Christina stared into her summer fire, thinking of Val.

After school, Christina slung her bookbag over her shoulder, careful not to squash Val's sandwich, and headed for the storm cottage. She was scarcely out the door when Robbie cornered her. "Christina!" he hissed in her ear. "Something terrible has happened."

"What?"

He cupped his hands around his lips and breathed in her ear. "Val is missing! My parents took me out of class fifth period to ask if I knew anything. They think she's run away, but I think the Shevvingtons have done away with her."

If she told Robbie that Val was fine, enjoying a storm cottage and freedom, Robbie would tell his parents, Mr. and Mrs. Armstrong would call an ambulance, and Val would be locked up in a hurry. "Robbie," she said nervously, wondering what kind of an actress she would be, "that's so scary. I'm so sorry." *Should I drop a clue?* she thought.

Benjamin arrived beside them. He elbowed Robbie out of the way. "I have to go to work," he said to Christina.

She nodded.

"But you can walk with me to the gas station," he said.

She nodded again.

Robbie flattened himself against the wall, looking miserable and helpless. Christina had an unworthy thought: Val had chosen to go to a stranger for help, not her own brother. Even lost, Val had known it was Christina who was made of granite. I'm granite of the Isle, thought Christina, and the whole middle school is watching Benj and me. She loved being the center of their attention. She paraded a little more.

Jonah and Robbie fell in step with them. Christina knew they were waiting for her to join them, talk to them, solve their problems for them. She said nothing. It was powerful: being silent when people wanted you to talk.

"Benj gave you his silence for your fourteenth birthday," teased Jonah. "Now he'll be with one who knows how to talk, Chrissie, and you'll be the silent Maine fisherman."

Benjamin ignored Jonah as too young and scrawny to count. "Astrid and Megan said they'd be happy to work with you," he said to Christina.

Robbie and Jonah faded away, like sails slipping from the shore. She felt herself stepping away from the entire seventh grade, moving up several years in several minutes.

For Benj's sake, she would not hold it against Astrid and Megan that they had abandoned Anya.

Perhaps they couldn't help it. Perhaps there were extenuating circumstances. Anyway, somebody as mature as Christina could forgive that sort of thing. She took Benj's hand and swung it.

"I got a B on an English paragraph today," he told her shyly.

She could not recall Benjamin Jaye ever mentioning an academic subject. Benj filled desk space, but he didn't actually do schoolwork. "That's wonderful," she said. "What was the paragraph about?"

Benjamin talked for several minutes as they walked down the blocks to his gas station. Why, he always had things to say, thought Christina. There just wasn't anybody listening!

At the gas station, however, Benj was the youngest. This changed him. His feet as well as his tongue stumbled. The other men grinned at Christina and looked knowingly at the clasped hands. Benjamin dropped her hand quickly to grip a toolbox instead.

"Little young, isn't she?" said an oil-stained man.

"I'm fourteen," said Christina with dignity.

The men all laughed, and Benj blushed. "Goodbye," he said, without looking at her. But she felt his heat.

He can't look at me, she thought. He's combustible: He'd catch fire. "Bye, Benj," she whispered, running off, escaping from the same fire: the fire that would consume them both. This is like when I had a crush on Blake! she thought, forgetting what pain that had brought her, remembering only the intense wonderful burning of love.

She meant to follow the shoreline to the storm cottage and get the food to Val. But she spotted Vicki and Gretch shopping in the boutiques that were beginning to open up for the tourist season. She went in another direction, and there, up the alley, was Robbie Armstrong coming toward her. She'd already talked to Robbie.

She ran again, taking the corners at full speed, bumping into tourists, and dashing between city cars. At the Town Hall she ducked in the lower entrance. There were public bathrooms and a drinking fountain; she would waste a little time there until the coast was clear and she could wend her way to the storm cottage and Val.

Across from the water fountain was an office whose sign read TOWN PERSONNEL. Christina frowned slightly. She considered the word "personnel" and what it meant. Then she walked in. Behind a counter made of rows of filing cabinets sat a gray-haired secretary. "Hello," said Christina.

The secretary smiled blankly. She seemed the kind of person who smiled well, but otherwise did nothing. Easy to con. "Um," began Christina, her head full of possibilities but none clear enough to surface. "Um," she said again. "There's going to be a surprise party," she said finally. "For the Shevvingtons. Do you know them? He's the principal and she teaches seventh-grade English."

"Oh, of course I know him. Such a fine man. I heard he's leaving our school system, though! What a loss to the town."

"A terrible loss," agreed Christina. "And the seventh grade is giving them a surprise good-bye party."

"How sweet! I didn't know children were still so sweet in this day and age."

"Well, they are," said Christina, who was not. "And what we want is guests from towns where the Shevvingtons used to teach. Before they came to Maine. So . . . um . . . I need a list of addresses. And it has to be a secret. Or the party won't be any fun. Promise?"

"I promise!" said the secretary gaily, and got right into the spirit of the thing, digging out addresses of schools where Mr. Shevvington had been principal before, and the names of the people who had written him recommendations. Mr. Shevvington had been in Louisiana and Pennsylvania, Oregon and New Jersey.

Christina slid the addresses into her bookbag. I've got it! she exulted. I've got a way to find out what they did before. I can locate the girls before Val! I can find out whose ghosts are locked into the first six guest rooms. I'm going to win. I'll save Val and not only that, I'll be saving all the girls who are out there, all unknowing, in the next town.

She said to the secretary, "This is so nice of you."

"I'd love to come to the party," said the secretary shyly.

"I'll send you an invitation," promised Christina. Party, she thought, hah! It's going to be a hanging.

Chapter 11

The long hills of Maine rippled like a Chinese dragon.

The sky grew dark. Fog bulged on the oceantop like the dragon's discarded skin; empty; ready to swallow victims.

Christina felt the sea dragon on her right side, curling forward over the waves. She felt the land dragon on her left, leaning through the trees and over the village.

She watched her feet instead, seeing her white sneakers grow wet as she wound among the rocks. She did not dare go on the upper path because summer people had come for the weekend, and they would leap forward the way summer people did, screaming, "What are you doing on my property!" Summer people were always frantic. They were always afraid of trespassers. They were always crying out, "I'll sue you!" instead of just getting a tan.

Christina scrambled among the smaller rocks below the seawall, exposed by the tide, where the dead horseshoe crabs lay among the dank seaweed and the barnacles scraped her skin.

Out at sea the wind increased. It took the fog in its arms and flung it toward Christina. It touched her bare arms and fondled her bare cheeks.

When she was below the storm cottage, she picked her way up the boulders to the rickety porch. The fog chased her ankles. She tilted open the shutter. "Val?" she hissed. She slid into the living room. The fog tried to follow. The wind came through the crack with her, lifting the white sheets on the furniture. The white walls waved, and the white floor shivered. But nobody answered.

"Val?" whispered Christina again.

How strange the house smelled. She paused in the whiteness of the rooms, sniffing. The smell was oily and cruel. It smelled of cities and gutters.

Something primitive, ancient and evil, crept up Christina's spine. The smell entered her nose and mouth, walked through her insides, and the entire world — all her flesh and all her soul — stank of the evil of it.

"*Val!*" she shouted.

What was the smell?

Had it sucked Val up?

She ran from room to room, and the smell ran with her. Every time her foot touched the floor she thought her sneaker sole might be eaten by acid.

Every breath she took, she thought her lungs would decay. *"Val! Where are you? Are you all right? I brought food!"*

The cottage was empty.

No one lay on the bare metal springs of the ugly old cots.

No one sat at the white porcelain table or opened the single drawer in the kitchen.

Val was gone.

Christina ran back to her window entrance.

The wind had thrown the shutter back and it was stuck fast.

She pushed and pulled at it, but its handles were on the outside. She ran to the other windows but they, too, were fastened from the outside. The smell grew thicker and stronger as if it were growing up from the cellar. Its appetite had increased. It liked little girls.

She flung herself into the tiny kitchen, and jumped up onto the counter. The tiny window over the old deep sink did not open. It never had, it never would. She jumped back down.

On the table — the tiny kitchen table — stood an old coffee can.

Inside the can tilted an old candle.

The candle was burning.

It was the can the Shevvingtons had left in her bedroom, the one she had tried to hide behind the geraniums. The one which had her fingerprints.

My fingerprints are on everything in this house,

thought Christina. And that smell — it's gasoline. This house is ready to burn.

From the depths of memory she heard Anya's voice. (Anya last fall, when the Shevvingtons began eating at her sanity.) "No, Chrissie," Anya had said, her hair a cloud of spun black glass. "The Shevvingtons will not destroy you. *You will destroy yourself.*"

Christina did not dare blow the flame out. There were enough gas fumes to light the kitchen. She wet her fingertips and squashed the flame. Racing back into the living room, she kicked the shutter open. The bottom hinge broke. It was no secret now; anybody could tell the storm cottage had been broken into.

And she knew, grimly, who would do the telling. The Shevvingtons.

And she knew who would produce the fingerprints for comparison. The Shevvingtons.

And she knew who would say, *But didn't we tell you she was nothing but a wharf rat?*

How had they known? How had they found out? Christina had told nobody!

She went out the window. The world was invisible. The fog was as thick as the inside of an envelope. The ocean she could not see chewed on the rocks she could not locate.

It was Anya's ocean; Anya had always said that at times like this, the sea sounded like a coffin being dragged over broken glass.

Whose coffin? thought Christina.

Mine?

Val's?

She ran, and the fog ran with her, engulfing her feet, swallowing the tips of her own fingers. She stumbled, but fog was no cushion. Rocks and barnacles ripped her skin. She cut between summer people's houses. The wet soggy branches of forsythia whipped her cheeks, and the heavy perfume of lilacs slapped her face. She slid on the grass and stained her clothes. At last she came out on the road, among headlights of cars, like dim yellow baskets.

Val, where are you? thought Christina. Are you safe? Did you go home? What happened?

She came into the village again and here the fog had come in soft and gray and cozy. Summer people were laughing at being lost only a few feet from each other. Natives were irritated and hoping it would sweep away soon.

Jonah was right, she thought. I got cocky. I was so sure of myself, so proud. He kept saying, *Pay attention, they're after you.* But would I listen to Jonah? No, because he's just in seventh grade and seventh-graders bore me.

A queer, horrible worry made her stop and look in her bookbag. She sat on a bench for tourists. Red geraniums nodded at her from out of the fog. She took out the sandwich. She took out the yogurt. She took out the apple. She took out her arithmetic book and her history book.

And yes.

There, beneath everything, caught in a seam, a lump so small only police fingers would have found it, was a box of matches.

Her hair was wet from the fog. No separate colors sprang from her head: no silver and gold, no rich chocolate-brown. Her hair was just a soggy mass, no different from anybody else's in the rain.

Nothing will save me, thought Christina Romney.

There will be a fire. The town will say that I set it. There will be fingerprints. The town will say I put them there. There will be a matchbox. The town will say I took it with me. They have forgotten the past. The memory of the village has been sealed up also.

They will catch me.

Mr. Shevvington's eyes will be soft and gray, like spring rain.

Mrs. Shevvington will nod her head like a guillotine in slow motion.

And the town will whisper, *We always knew she was just a wharf rat.*

Chapter 12

The fog began whispering. The whisper was thick and snuffly and damp. *"The alone,"* it breathed. *"The alone."*

It was the voice of Christina's fears: that one day she would be alone . . . all alone . . . the world would end . . . while she wandered . . . her breathing the only breathing on earth . . . her footsteps the only footsteps on earth. *The alone.*

Mattresses of fog disappeared when she walked through them.

The alone, repeated the world.

Fear struck Christina's lungs, and she breathed in the fog itself, lungs heaving as if she were in a track race. The fog sat in her lungs like a wet towel, suffocating her.

And now the fog murmured *Chhhrrrisssssteee-nnnaaaaaaaahhhh*, and she knew it had come for her; it was going to wrap its wet arms around her; it would take her —

"I was afraid of *the alone*," said Val clearly, and

now Christina could see her: slim and damply pretty, blending with the tourists. "The storm cottage," said Val, clinging to Christina, her fingers like tree toads plastered to Christina's arms. "It was so full of *alone*. I was alone, it was alone, the sea was alone, the sheets on the chairs were alone. Christina, I couldn't bear it."

Christina tried to peel Val off but Val was too afraid of *the alone* to let go. Her fingers are just fingers, Christina told herself, not toads.

"The Shevvingtons called the fog in," said Val. "I heard them. They were in the storm cottage and they called to the fog, and the fog answered and obeyed."

Christina shuddered convulsively. She could imagine their arms, their curled fingers, their furry voices. "The fog was coming in anyway, Val," said Christina. "They weren't calling it. They don't have special powers."

"Of course they do," said Val. "I knew once the fog came in, the alone would have me, and the Shevvingtons would have me and it would be over. They stood on the rocks outside the storm cottage and held their hands up to the ocean, laughing, and the ocean laughed with them, and all together they cried, '*Fog. Fog. Fog.*'"

I knew they were in the storm cottage, thought Christina. I knew they were the ones who spilled . . .

Her thoughts bumped into a terrible wall. A wall of sharp spikes and knife-edged wire. A wall of Evil.

Gasoline. Matches. Val.

"No," said Christina, as if to stop Evil with a syllable. "The Shevvingtons are terrible people, but setting fire to the storm cottage while you were in it? Even the Shevvingtons wouldn't —"

"Yes, they would," said Val. "I'm starving, Christina. Did you bring me anything to eat?"

Christina handed over the sandwich. Val tore off the wrapper and ate savagely. Christina pictured the sandwich still whole lying in Val's stomach.

I told Benj to believe in Evil, thought Christina, but here I am facing Evil, and I don't believe. People don't really do things like that. Not just for the fun of it. Because there's no reason except entertainment. There's no money, no power, no status. "But why?" whispered Christina. "Why would they plan that?"

"Because there aren't enough days left," said Val. "You keep outwitting them, Christina. That's dumb. If you would just be dumb yourself, they wouldn't care about getting you, too. They were gloating, because they could get both of us forever. They said it would be a pleasant finale to a difficult year. That was their word. Pleasant. They said it would be pleasant to wrap things up. Meaning you. Do you have anything else to eat?"

Christina gave her the apple. I bet she eats the core, too, thought Christina, and she was right.

Christina's head throbbed hideously. So this is what a real headache is, she thought. It bites from the inside. It chews on your eyes and your brain and the hearing parts of your ears.

"We have to call the fire department before the gasoline catches," she said dully. "Or they'll blame me." Christina started crying. She thought of the storm cottage, and the innocent summer people whose place would go up in flames, and all because — as Benj would have been the first to tell her — she had trespassed for the fun of it. "They'll blame me anyway. I'll be the one calling the fire department, and my fingerprints are all over the place." Christina could not imagine what her mother and father and Benj and Jonah and Vicki and Gretch and everybody else on earth would have to say.

And then she could imagine.

Perfectly.

Wharf rat, they would say, their pointing fingers jabbing into her chest. Wharf rat, wharf rat, wharf rat!

Val shook her head. "Chrissie, I didn't have anything else to do waiting for you to come back, so I scrubbed everything you had touched. And you carried the coffee can and the candle away with you." Val grubbed in the bookbag, hoping for more to eat, and found the yogurt. She used two bent fingers for a spoon and slurped it up. She said, "Anyhow, while they summoned the fog, I slid out the cellar window."

"I'm impressed, Val. I thought you'd be insane."

"I was for a while. The alone really got to me. But you're here now. I'm leaning on you, and I'm fine. Where are you going to hide me now?"

Christina knew more or less where they were,

but the fog that had hidden Val from Christina's sight could hide listeners and enemies, too: the Shevvingtons need stand only a few yards away and they, too, would be swallowed in the thick gray fog.

The passage to the sea, thought Christina. The cliff passage where the Shevvingtons' horrible insane son slipped back and forth unseen so he could terrorize Anya. The sea opened it up again. I heard it crash through last night.

Generations ago, the sea captain had built in that strange location, where the high tide coming into Candle Cove made the house shake with every thundering wave. Nobody knew why he chose that cliff edge. And then Christina had found out why: He must have been smuggling something in or out his hidden hole. You could reach it only at low tide. At high tide, it was covered by water. How well she knew that cellar. The mold that grew on the walls; the smell of the tide lodged in the cracks; the cold, watery drafts that slid around your ankles. She remembered how the horrible passage tilted into the water, and she had once been forced down it, while the *thing*, the unknowable, rubbery, inhuman thing, had laughed madly from above. The thing that was the Shevvingtons' son.

She could imagine herself in that passage again — and the Shevvingtons cementing it up on both sides while she was trying to hide Val there.

No, the cliff passage was not a possibility.

"I can't go back to the storm cottage," quavered

Val. She shuddered and grabbed Christina's hand. "The alone would get me."

Christina could not loosen Val's grip. She had the impression that if Val did not hang onto her, Val would tip over. Val was literally, as well as mentally, unbalanced.

The full horror of it struck Christina. Val *needed* the care and the help of professionals. She needed the love and the knowledge of people who helped the mentally distraught. She probably needed her mother. It couldn't be good for Val to be by herself, surrounded by white sheets and booming tides, wondering if *the alone* was going to get her.

The fog began to curl back away from the coast, as if the gods of the sea — of the Shevvingtons — were peeling it away. They could see twenty feet ahead of them, and then a hundred feet.

The Atlantic burbled and chuckled like a nursery school playgroup.

Far out on the horizon, a fire blazed. Gaudy strips of flame pierced the fog. Glowing embers of ship or house. Burning Fog Isle, up to its old tricks with the prism of fog and sun.

I want to go home, thought Christina. I want my mother. I want my father. I want everything the way it used to be, all safe and cozy.

She could telephone her parents. "Mommy, remember how Anya almost lost her mind, and the year before, Robbie's sister Val did lose hers and had to be put away? Val ran away from the Institute and came to me because I went there under a false name to visit her because I needed information against the Shevvingtons. The Shevvingtons know that I know about them, and they have very little time to destroy me. They are planning to set fire to the storm cottage where I've been hiding Val, and they will make it look as if I did it. They've been putting matches and candles everywhere I go. They are going to blame me for arson, Mommy! I'll be a wharf rat before I'm even in high school."

And her parents would say — as they wept — "No nice, kind adult like dear Mr. Shevvington would do that. It must be something about the way we brought her up, out here on this island, without a normal twentieth-century social life; it must be our fault. Christina really did do it herself."

And yet . . . if Christina did *not* tell, Val might slip into the alone, and never come out.

Chapter 13

"*Stay here?*" cried Val. "Oh, no, Chrissie, no, I — "

"Here," said Christina firmly.

"Impossible," breathed Val. "I'll go insane."

They giggled desperately. Room 7 swirled around them, crimson and dark violet, crystal clear and dusk-quiet.

"I'll be in and out," promised Christina.

"But Chrissie." Val was gasping for breath. "Chrissie, it's their plan." Her voice became softer, tinier. "For me to come here. I can feel it. *The Shevvingtons know.*"

"They do not know. And you can get away with it, Val, I know you can. The first rule of hiding something is to put it right out in the open where it belongs. Like the best place to hide a car is a big parking lot, not a backyard."

"This room isn't big."

"It's yours, though, Val. It was decorated for you."

"It's my shell. You said so yourself."

"You'll find yourself in here, Val. You'll go back to being the old Val."

Val's laugh was high and broken, like the top of an electric keyboard, losing its current. "My ghost lives here. *The alone* lives here."

"The Shevvingtons'll be at school during the day. You can eat and go to the bathroom and watch television. And if there are cookies gone or something — why, three teenagers eat here, anyway. What do they expect? Besides, they'd never think to look for you here, Val. They'd expect you to run as far from them as you could."

The sun had moved over Schooner Inne to the west, town-facing side of the house. Room 7 looked out on an ocean not blue, nor green, but kitten-gray. Soft, fuzzy, wet gray. The sky dissolved like aspirin in a glass, and you could not tell the horizon from the ocean.

"It's too bleak," Val whispered. "I've always been afraid of the ocean. It's so noisy. It yells at me. Calls my name." Val pulled the window shades down and yanked the crimson curtains shut.

"You shouldn't do that," said Christina. "That's evidence. If they look in this guest room, and they will, because they gloat every day, they'll see the curtains have been moved."

"They look in here every day? You put me on purpose in a room the Shevvingtons look in every day?"

Christina twitched the curtains back and yanked

the shade up again. Against the aspirin sky, a dark thundercloud began to form.

"Chrissie, don't do that. I can't have an open window where things can look in at me. That cloud is pointing straight at me."

"There's nothing out there but cliff and air," said Christina. "The only thing that could look at you is a sea gull."

"They called the fog," said Val. "They could call a sea gull. They could come as sea gulls. They could float in on the tide, like *the alone*. Like the fog."

"Don't be ridiculous," said Christina. "Get a grip on yourself."

Val laughed again. It sounded like a tourist, somebody from a pickup truck throwing a glass bottle against the sidewalk. Tourists loved to break glass.

Will this break Val? thought Christina. But there isn't anyplace else. I can't take her back to the storm cottage. The Shevvingtons —

— *were planning even now to set fire to the storm cottage*. Where they expected Val to be. They had to be stopped. "Remember my rules," said Christina fiercely to Val, and she ran back down the stairs.

In the dim half-light of the front hall, with the forest of white-carved banisters curling above her, she began dialing the phone. Nine, one, one. Her fingers shook. The phone seemed remarkably heavy.

Above her, on the middle landing, Val leaned over the railing. "I'm dizzy, Chrissie," she muttered. "It's dizzy up here." If Val fainted, she'd do a swan dive down the stairs.

"Emergency," said a solid, sure voice. The kind of voice that knew how to do things with hoses and ladders and horrors. It had a heavy Maine accent: almost an island voice. A voice whose twang spelled comfort and safety to Christina Romney.

"I need help," said Christina, and the moment she admitted it, her own voice broke and she burst into tears.

"I'm here," said the voice, "don't panic. Tell me where you are and what the emergency is."

On the upstairs balcony, Val began sobbing in harmony with her. It was eerie, like weeping through stereo speakers. "There isn't a fire yet," said Christina, struggling to control the sobs. I can't break down, she thought, I've been so strong so far. "I was playing house in a summer cottage. A storm cottage up the shore. I know I shouldn't have been there. But when I went up today, somebody had splashed gasoline all over the house. I think they're going to set fire to it." Did she dare tell the good twanging Maine voice that the Shevvingtons were going to set the fire? The principal everybody loved versus the mad little island girl whose pockets were stuffed with matches? "Please — please — " What am I saying *please* for? wondered Christina as she said it. Please save me? Please save Val? Please end this?

The voice was slow and easy. It coaxed Christina to give her name and location, the address of the storm cottage, the number of times she had played in the house.

Val crept down the carpeted stairs, sidled up to Christina, and stood with her head pressed against Christina's thick hair, soaking up equal comfort from the voice inside the phone. "Go back upstairs and hide," hissed Christina.

Val shook her head. "Too scary up there."

A few moments later they heard sirens, but the voice kept on talking. "You're a good brave girl, Christina," said the voice. "You did the right thing. I'm a friend of your parents, did you know that? I'm Jimmy Gardner; I went to high school with your mom. I'm in the fire department. Volunteer, of course. My real job's running the cannery."

The cannery. Wharf rats. Empty shells.

"Now you stay on the phone with me. I had somebody get on another line and call your school. Mr. Shevvington is coming right down to be with you. He'll be kind and understanding. He's a fine man."

Christina began laughing.

"Don't get hysterical on me," said Mr. Gardner. "You've been calm so far. You probably prevented arson. We had some trouble with that last year in empty houses, and we certainly don't want it again this year." He paused, but Christina had nothing to say.

The front door to Schooner Inne opened.

Val leaped backwards, falling into the parlor with the cold fire.

Mr. Shevvington filled the hall. Today's three-piece suit was a deep, rich, navy blue. One of the colors of Val's room. Had he seen Val? Did he already know? Would he tell Mr. Gardner to send an ambulance for Val as well?

Mr. Shevvington took the phone out of Christina's hands. "I'm here, Jim," he said into the receiver. "Good of you to handle her so gently. Poor Christina often does not entirely understand what is going on."

His mad blue eyes rotated in his head as if they had come unattached. He was not only insane-mad; right now he was furious-mad. His fingers dug into Christina like lobster claws until she cried out in pain. In sympathy, Val moaned behind the parlor door.

The phone mumbled.

"Your wife is what?" repeated Mr. Shevvington into the phone. "Your wife is the personnel secretary?"

Christina went limp. It was easy to forget what a small town this was; how everybody knew everybody, or was married to somebody's cousin, or had been to school with somebody.

"And Christina was in the personnel office getting addresses of my previous schools? For a surprise party?" Mr. Shevvington's lips began to curl back away from his teeth. They drew out into a horrible lifted oval, so all his teeth pointed at her.

He began bending over her, bringing his twisted face closer and closer to hers. Christina shrank back against the flocked wallpaper. Through the crack of the door Val's single brown eye watched in horror.

"But your wife asked other seventh-graders and there was no surprise party planned?" Mr. Shevvington straightened up. The lips closed again and then folded over, making several smiles — a whole series of smiles — like evil plans. "Why, Jim, how thoughtful of you to become concerned. And of course, you are so intuitive, you and your dear wife . . . yes . . . poor Christina . . . you're absolutely right, these island children are ingrown . . . warped . . . a sort of wharf rat mentality . . . frightening in certain ways . . . thank you for telling me . . . my wife and I will certainly bear this in mind."

He hung up.

The storm cottage was safe.

But Christina and Val were not.

Chapter 14

Christina could hear the double breathing. Her own shallow and moist; Val's quick and dry. It seemed impossible that Mr. Shevvington did not hear both girls.

It was on Christina alone that his hands tightened, and his fury mounted.

She tried to get the telephone back, to call 911 again.

"And what would you say?" asked Mr. Shevvington sweetly. "Dear Mr. Gardner, I think Mr. Shevvington is annoyed with me! Please send help."

Christina bit him.

It was the most disgusting thing she had ever done in her life. Even the time two summers ago when Michael dared her to eat a jellyfish raw from the beach, and she did, it had not been so disgusting. She was the one who screamed, not Mr. Shevvington. He yanked his hand back and stared at her.

"I'm rabid," Christina told him. "You'll need shots. Right in the stomach. Hundreds of them."

The doorbell rang.

Mr. Shevvington looked at his watch and muttered to himself. Quickly he wrapped her tooth marks in his handkerchief. He always wore a lovely silk hanky whose tips decorated his lapel pocket. The crimson and royal-blue paisley seemed stolen from Val's room. "It's a potential buyer," he mumbled. "A couple coming to look at the Inne."

Christina smiled. "I'll be sure to tell them what it's really like here."

But when the door opened, before Mr. Shevvington could go to answer it, Robbie and his mother peeked into the front hall. Christina squeaked. Behind her door Val swallowed as loud as an engine. The thunderstorm that had been brewing between the island and the coast, broke. Rain came down in sweeping torrents. Val could lie down and groan now and nobody would hear, thought Christina. They would still see, however.

"Come in, come in," said Mr. Shevvington testily, worried now about his wallpaper and his carpet getting wet.

Mrs. Armstrong looked like Val, but haggard — the way Val's grandmother ought to look. The Shevvingtons did that, thought Christina. They aged her, when they chose Val to ruin.

"We haven't found a trace of Val. Can you think of anyplace else to look?"

Mr. Shevvington put his good arm around her shoulder, protectively cradling his bitten hand. "Poor, poor Genevieve," he said.

So that was her name. It was a good name for her. Gentle and old.

Genevieve wept. Not the lumpy crying of Christina's panic with Mr. Gardner. Nor the homesick tears that had drenched her pillow at the beginning of the school year. But old tears, as if she were recycling them from a previous disaster.

Val won't be able to stand this, thought Christina. She'll come out from behind the door. I would, too, in her place. Her mother needs her. Anyway, any institution would be less risky than the Shevvingtons.

"My father's driving around town," Robbie said. "He thinks maybe he'll find her hitchhiking."

"Poor, poor Alan," said Mr. Shevvington. His eyes were half hidden under folded lids, as if he were resting in there, swinging in a hammock, enjoying himself.

Why, he has two extra victims I didn't even know about, realized Christina. He uses their first names to make them littler, younger. Because that's what he's reduced them to: They're hardly more than seventh-graders themselves. Genevieve and Alan. Not Mr. and Mrs. Armstrong. Not grown-ups.

One good thing: Val was only a few feet away. Either she would surrender or she wouldn't. The choice was no longer Christina's.

"They've explained to us," said Val's mother sadly, "that Val has to spend her life at the Institute. We have to get her back there."

"Her *life!*" cried Christina. "She's only seventeen."

Robbie shrugged. "There's no other answer."

"There has to be another answer," said Christina.

"Robbie, let's go, honey," said his mother, sagging. "I don't know why we came here, really. Except we've been everywhere else."

"I'll walk you to your car," said Mr. Shevvington, opening the door again. The rain was even heavier. He hoisted a huge British umbrella and held it over Mrs. Armstrong.

"Oh, Arnold, you're so kind," she wept. She leaned on him as they went down the granite steps, crossed Breakneck Hill Road, and stopped at the old economy-model Ford.

Christina jerked Val out from behind the parlor door. "Run upstairs!" she hissed. "If they're showing the house to buyers, they'll look everywhere. Hide in your room."

Val wouldn't budge. "They'll look there, too, Chrissie. Did you hear what my mother said? My own mother? She is going to lock me up forever. And I'm only seventeen."

"The Shevvingtons probably told an all-new set of stories about you. Probably convinced the whole staff whatever it is is true. We'll get you away. *Just hurry up the stairs.*"

Val was thin from her hospital stay. Her skinny little legs churned up the long staircase.

As thin as Dolly, thought Christina, or as Anya

when she was at her most faded. Perhaps food and energy is the real key to keeping sane. So I'll be sure to have a big dinner. Plenty of roast beef.

Knowing Mrs. Shevvington they would be having eggplant lasagne instead. Ugh.

Mr. Shevvington came back in. Gently he shook the umbrella. Gracefully he closed it, setting it to drain in the elegant Chinese vase the sea captain had brought back from his voyages to the Orient. Mr. Shevvington's smile peaked and valleyed on his face like the crest of a wave. Christina moved down the hall, to a place where she had several choices: kitchen, back door, stairs. "So, Christina of the Isle," he said softly, "where is our little Valerie?"

"Val? I haven't even met her. She's been in an institution since I came on the mainland, remember?"

The evil inside Mr. Shevvington glowed. She could see it through his skin: lanterns of it. If she touched his glow, would it be hot or cold? Would it, once touched, pass into her body, too, like an electrical current? Turning even Christina of the Isle into someone evil?

Upstairs a door snicked shut. Mr. Shevvington did not appear to hear it. The hand she had bitten came toward her. The paisley silk kerchief dangled on it like a flag over a coffin. The blue eyes fell down, as if unhinged, and the lobster claw fingers caught the fabric of Christina's shirt.

Christina did not dare leave Val alone — but she could not stay here, either.

Val was on her own.

Christina tore loose. She burst out the door into the pouring rain and ran to the gas station. The rain soaked her. The thunder jarred her joints. Lightning bristled in the sky like rocket launches. I'll get Benjamin, she thought. He's safe, he's strong. I'll tell him, he'll know what to do.

With the confusing abruptness of summer storms, the rain moved on up the coast to attack other towns. The sun came back out, the ocean turned blue-green again, and the road surfaces steamed. Christina sprinted through puddles and splashed herself with mud. I probably look about ten years old, she thought. And I still have teary-red eyes. What will Benjamin think of me?

It was the first time in her life she had really wondered what a boy would think of her looks. Or cared.

Christina ran through the empty lot behind the gas station. Tall weeds brushed her legs. A small white butterfly fled from her thrashing feet. Behind the garage was a car storage yard, fenced like a prison. Barbed wire curled on top. Far above, in the suddenly blue sky, was a bird, floating.

Benjamin! Benjamin!

She planned to fling herself on him, tell him everything, stand still while he solved it.

But Benjamin was surrounded by tourists, expecting him to fix their cars. All her island training rose up: She must not look demented in front of tourists. They were lifeblood; they were money. She slowed, donning her "Welcome, Tourist" face.

How pleased Benjamin was to see her. Why, even as disheveled as she was, she had only to walk up, and his face lit up in a smile so handsome, so fine, that she wanted to keep it for her very own. A smile he'd kept secret for just this: a girl.

I'm the girl, marveled Christina. She stood in the shade of a maple tree, behind a wreck recently towed in by the state police. She was glad she was turning fourteen soon. Thirteen seemed too young for love. Her parents would not like it.

"Be with you in a minute," said Benj. "I have to change the belts on this car."

How impatient the tourists were. Christina had a fine eye for tourists. Before she was two years old, she could tell a tourist from an islander. Now she preferred finer divisions. Boston or New York? Michigan or Mississippi? She murmured the question to Benj. "I don't divide them that way," he said.

"How do you divide them?" she asked.

"Dragged and undragged."

Christina pictured a fisherman's net hauled along the ocean floor, gathering scallops and tourists. But she did not understand.

"The ones who want to come on vacation, and the ones who are dragged," explained Benj.

Christina checked them out. Sure enough, the man wanted to be on vacation and the woman did not. The wife would have liked to be back in whatever city she came from, making money, being important. Her husband just wanted to be sailing. Well, it was possible to combine these things on the coast of Maine. Christina almost said to them, "Want to buy an inn?"

"Yep," said Benjamin, actually laughing out loud. "Dragged and undragged. Like school." (Benj was definitely dragged to school.)

"Think Disney World," said Christina.

Benjamin, hands black with oil, coveralls stained, cheek smeared, smiled again. His smile lit her heart like a match. "Think sophomore dance," he said.

And so she told Benj nothing.

For it dawned on Christina that she did not know Benjamin Jaye at all. Who would have guessed that his heart was full of romance and his soul yearned for love? She would have said his heart beat only for fishing; that his soul never noticed anything, except whether it was low tide.

Perhaps nobody knows anybody, thought Christina.

It was a terrifying thought: like *the alone*. That you could know people well, and know them again the following year, and then know them more . . . and yet remain strangers forever.

Chapter 15

Christina sat on the open back of the garage's pick-up truck, swinging her feet above the pavement, waiting for Benj. Her feet were bare and dusty in her narrow leather sandals. In the stiff breeze, her thin skirt swirled and unswirled around her legs like pink cotton candy spun onto the white paper cylinder.

"That little girl looks like the figurehead on a sailing ship," said the tourist woman to her husband.

Christina liked that, and kept her chin high, bending her small wrists into the air as if she were a prow, cutting through the Atlantic. Finally there was a moment of quiet at the garage, and Benj perched on the edge of the truck with her. His legs dangled, too, but he did not swing them. Benj was not a swinger, not of legs and not of life. She said, "My mother's coming in on Frankie's boat tomorrow. We'll go shopping for a dress for the dance."

Benj said, "I don't know what I should wear."

"What's everybody else wearing?" asked Christina immediately.

Benj smiled slightly. "Chrissie Romney," he said, "I didn't think you cared what anybody else did."

"For clothes I do. If you go to a dance in the wrong things you won't have any fun, that's all. What did the other boys say they were wearing?"

"They didn't say."

"Ask them."

Benj shrugged. "I don't want to talk about dumb things like that."

"I'll ask, then. Who shall I ask? I don't know any other sophomores."

"But you did ask your parents if it's all right, didn't you?" said Benj anxiously.

"Of course. They think it's neat." Christina smiled at him, and to her surprise he ducked his head, staring at the mess of car parts and broken tools and pieces off things that leaned against the side of the garage. We're flirting, she thought. I bet no other seventh-grade girl is practicing to flirt right now. It's because I'm so mature. It's my island granite. And after all, he's only two years and a few months older.

She was seized by joy. She jumped up into the bed of the pickup, with its corrugated metal bottom, and began dancing. "Dance with me," she commanded him, but of course he didn't. He told her to stop, because she looked weird, you weren't supposed to dance in trucks.

Christina stopped. But not because you weren't

supposed to dance in trucks. Because a short, heavy man with a thick, bristly beard and a big barrel chest was coming toward her. He waved in a friendly way. He said, "Christina? Say, I'm glad to meet you."

Christina was normally very friendly to strangers. She loved strangers. But this was no tourist; she who knew her tourists knew he was a local. But unknown to her. She felt a strange quiver of suspicion. Why had he parked, blocking the garage? Why was he striding over like this? Who —?

"Jim Gardner," he said, a smile peeking out from behind the beard. There was too much hair over the smile to tell if it was a real smile or a fake smile: It was just a flash of teeth. He stuck his hand out. He had a huge hand, much bigger than he should have had for his body. The hand gave Christina the creeps, and when she shook it, the hot dry skin felt like a reptile's. He hung onto her too long, as if he planned on keeping her. "Hi, Benj," he said in a familiar way.

"Jim," nodded Benj.

The man turned immediately away from Benjamin. His face was eye level to her dancing legs. "Christina, honey, I wonder if you and I could have a little talk. About the Shevvingtons. About the storm cottage."

Benj swung around to look Christina in the eyes. She was above him, too, in the truckbed. "What storm cottage?" said Benj, frowning.

It made her so mad! The Shevvingtons weren't coming after her themselves; they were sending Another Authority. Someone nobody questioned, even Benjamin Jaye. He was already prepared to assume Christina was in the wrong. "My storm cottage," she said brightly, "the one I sneak into sometimes. I told Mr. Gardner about it. There's nothing more to say. I won't trespass any more." Christina hated to apologize. The worst sentence in English was "I'm sorry." She forced herself to spit it out, even though she wasn't sorry and would never be sorry. "I'm sorry." She did not sound sorry. She sounded as if she would like to throw dirt in their faces. Her parents would never let her get away with that tone of voice, but Mr. Gardner and Benj didn't know what to do about it.

Christina backed up against the cab of the truck, leaned on the rusting red paint, and folded her arms over her chest.

"Christina, you have to believe I'm your friend in this," said Mr. Gardner. He took hold of the side of the truck. His smile came back and stayed beneath the beard, little bits of white tooth sticking out, as if his teeth weren't attached, merely sprinkled into the beard.

He's here to take me away! she thought. The Shevvingtons said I was insane. A crazy wharf rat. Plays with matches. "You think I need a friend right now?" she said nervously.

He vaulted up into the truck with her and came

closer, slowly, as if she were dangerous.

She held up her hands, flat, like a barricade. "Don't touch me."

"Chrissie," said Benj blankly, "what's going on? Nobody's going to touch you. What are you afraid of? Mr. Gardner's an old friend of your parents'."

The air was humid, and the world hummed.

"All we need is a little talk, Chrissie," said Mr. Gardner in a slow, soothing voice. An attendant's voice. A white-uniformed guard's voice. It oiled its way across the truck, even as his shoes slid across the truck, getting closer and closer. His hands were out, too, ready to grab her wrists. He had his car parked like that to block her escape. Probably his car had no handles on the inside. Probably once she was in that car, she was in it forever.

Like Val.

At seventeen, her own mother agreeing to shut her up forever. Forever. Forever. Christina backed into the far corner. It was not a large truck. There was not much corner. "Leave me alone."

"I have to talk to you, Christina," he said. His voice was silky, like all enclosures, like all traps.

Christina. Child of wind and sand, tides and isles. "No, don't lock me up!" she screamed. "I can't stand it!" She jumped over the edge of the truck, landing lightly on her sandals. Benj circled the truck to grab her. Mr. Gardner jumped off after her.

"I'm your parents' friend!" shouted Mr. Gardner, coming after her. "Don't be afraid of me."

She had never run so fast. She had not known

she was capable of running so fast. She reached the sidewalk and saw the Shevvingtons' van at the other end of the street. They had blocked her off. They were on all sides.

The only sounds on earth were the smacking of Christina's sandals on pavement and the heaving of her lungs. In silence the Shevvingtons lunged for her, in silence Mr. Gardner chased her, in silence Benjamin tried to cut her off.

In the west, the sun chose an angle that was piercing and harsh. Christina's hair was on fire with it, melting. She felt the heat, felt her separate colors, and then — no color at all. They've come for me and taken my color, thought Christina. I'll be white, like the sheets in the storm cottage and the uniforms at the Institute.

Her feet slapped the pavement. Wharf, rat, wharf, rat, wharf, rat, wharf, said the rhythm of her running.

Up Breakneck Hill she ran; through the thick green doors of Schooner Inne; into the cold silent house where Evil lived. She bolted the doors behind her, so nobody could get in: nobody, no matter how many keys they carried and how well they called the fog.

She took the stairs two at a time. She flung open the door to her bedroom: the guest room of fire and isles. It was empty. She flung open the door to guest room number 7: the room of Val, of crimson and violet. It was empty. Empty in the closet, empty under the bed, empty in the blanket chest, empty behind the curtains. "Val!" screamed Christina. "Val, where are you? We have to go!"

She ran up to the third floor to her old room, with its peeling paint and its single dark window. It was empty. The mattress was stripped. The posters were gone. The lamp had no bulb. "Val! Val!" shrieked Christina. "They're coming! We have to go!"

She looked in the boys' room. She looked in the room that Dolly and Anya had once shared. She looked in the cupola.

Empty. Empty. Empty.

Like our souls, thought Christina. Like all the girls before us.

She ran down the stairs, ran down and down and down among the forest of white banisters, while the house whispered, *Chhhhhrrrrrisssssstina! Chhhhrrrrisssssstina!* The tide slammed against the foundations and the house rocked. Her heart and soul rocked with it, shaken inside her ribs, thrown against her hope. She ran through the hall, she tore through the kitchen, she ripped open the cellar door. "Val, where are you?"

Brown hair emerged from the floor. Insane brown eyes stared out of pale, scared skin.

"Val?" whispered Christina.

But it was not Val. It had fingers like Val, and bones like Val, and skin like Val, but there was no person inside it. Its eyes flew around like small birds.

"It's me," whispered Christina.

Val slithered out like an animal and crawled up to Christina, making little whimpery noises. Her touch was clammy and damp, like frogs.

"*The alone*," said Val. "The alone got me."

Christina could feel *the alone*. It was under the house, hot and panting. It was up the stairs, crouching and sucking. It was in the air, ghostly and sightless.

FfffffFFFFFFF*FFFFFF*, said the house.

FfffffFFFFFFF*FFFFFF*, said the sea.

I am granite of the Isle, she reminded herself. I am Christina Romney and I am afraid of nothing. "I'm here now. You're not alone." I'm lying, she thought. When I first came here, Mr. Shevvington wanted me to make a list of all the things I am afraid of. For his Fear Files. I remember Anya filled it out. But I wouldn't do it. I didn't want him to know what I'm afraid of. But he knew anyway. He knew before I ever got to Schooner Inne.

Val's eyes widened.

"I am not afraid," said Christina. But she was afraid. She was afraid of being alone, and unloved, and unwanted. She was afraid of falling backward, of the Shevvingtons' plans.

Val's eyes grew wider still: holes for Christina to fall in. "I will always be alone," she said. Her voice was dead and lost.

"No," said Christina loudly. She felt that the louder they talked, the more she could scare off *the alone*. "Come back, Val. You're not alone. I'm here." She dragged Val into the kitchen but she could go no further. She felt as if she had dragged Val a hundred miles.

They fell into chairs at the table. The room had the thick, dull heat of closed-up rooms in summer. The only cheerful spot in the entire dreary kitchen was a bowl of oranges in the center of the table. Christina lifted one as if it were a leaden weight. "Here. Let's have an orange." She knew they should be running. The Shevvingtons, Mr. Gardner, and Benj were on their way, closing in. But she could not move. She was sapped of energy. Is this what a maple tree feels like when they tap its juices? she thought. Is the tree tired and its leaves droopy and then rooted forever to one place and can never move on?

Val stared at the round, bright fruits as if they were unknown to her; as if they grew on other planets, in other eons. "No, thank you," she said.

Trees can't move on anyway, thought Christina. I'm definitely going insane. But I have to get Val out of *the alone* first.

Christina felt it: *The alone* came up from the cellar on the sea wind, full of damp and decay. It touched her bare ankles and crept up her bare legs. She tried to brush it off, like insects, and it swarmed around her jackhammering head, like wasps.

I'm half here, she thought. Like being half in the water. My tide is rising. Or is it ebbing? Where is the rest of me? Drowning?

"I'll peel one for you," Christina offered. She dug her fingernails into the orange peel, and the air suddenly smelled of citrus: It was a sharp, tangy, good smell. It killed off *the alone* that was lingering by their shoulders, touching their hair. "Doesn't it smell wonderful?" said Christina, holding it up, wafting it around like incense.

A smile touched Val's lips. "It smells like Christmas." She touched the orange skin lightly with one finger, exploring memories. "And all the things I don't have anymore," she said sadly.

"But they'll come back now, Val," said Christina. "You'll be well and everything good will be yours."

Val laughed. Her laugh was bright and brittle. It had a crack in it, like an old piece of pottery. She looked at Christina as an ancient crone looks at innocence. "No," said Val. "I think when you've lost childhood, you've lost it forever."

Chapter 16

"Chrissie," said Val. Her lovely eyes were half hidden by falling lids almost transparent: The tiny veins were maps of blue.

You can see right through her, thought Christina. "What, Val?" She felt like taking a nap. Or two naps. She had never been so tired in her life. She wondered if her eyes looked like Val's. How did sleep restore eyelids?

Val leaned forward, so limp and exhausted she folded down over the table and the orange peels. "They know I'm here."

"Who knows?"

"The Shevvingtons."

"They do not! If they knew, they'd turn you in."

Val shook her head. "Cats don't always kill the mouse, you know. Sometimes they catch it in their teeth and shake it around, and drop it, and let it run a few feet, and then catch it again."

Christina's big, old house and barn on the island had a dozen cats, and perhaps a thousand mice. She knew cats and mice. She said, "Did the Shevvingtons see you in here, Val?"

"No. But they laughed. The way they did each time they visited me at the Shoreline Institute. Gloating. Knowing."

In the hot, still, musty house Christina began shivering.

"Mrs. Shevvington purrs," said Val.

The house closed in on them like an envelope, sealing them in with the stickiness of Mrs. Shevvington.

"I lay under the bed in my room," said Val, "and the bedcovers draped down so low I was completely hidden. They stood in the doorway and laughed like leopards. Furry and spotted. Then they went downstairs and lit a fire in the fireplace. I got out from under the bed and I ran into your room Christina."

"Which of my rooms?"

"The attic."

"There's no place to hide in there."

"There's a blanket chest. I got in there and shut the lid on myself."

"You could have suffocated!"

"It doesn't close that tight. I checked first. Anyway, the Shevvingtons were showing the Inne to a couple who wanted to buy it and when they got up to the second balcony, they looked in the empty room that Anya and Dolly used to have, and they looked in the room that Michael and Benj share — but they stood outside your door, Chrissie, and they laughed, and they said to the couple, 'This is just like the other rooms, but we haven't cleaned it out yet. There are things in it we're going to throw away.' "

The girls looked at each other.

Things in it the Shevvingtons were going to throw away.

"Us," whispered Val.

As if they had not listened to earlier, softer, warnings, the tide began slamming against the house. It pounded and pounded, like fists on wood. "When I was in the cellar," Val whispered, "the house called your name, Chrissie. I think they'll throw you away first."

Christina's head throbbed. She could no longer tell if the noise was the tide, or the world, or her own brain. I need earplugs, she thought. Unless all the noise is really me, in which case I need an ice-cream scoop, to scoop it all out of my head.

What a weird idea. Perhaps this was the way people went insane. They decided they didn't want the insides of their heads anymore and scooped it out like ice cream and let it all melt.

She was going in and out of her mind like a cartoon character caught in a revolving door. Briefly Christina swung into her mind and her mind rushed on, dumping her somewhere else.

Chhhhhrrrrrrisssssssstina, said the house.

Come, Chhhhrrrrrrisssssssstina.

Crazy, thought Christina. I'm going crazy.

She stood up and walked away, as if crazy were a destination: a seat at the kitchen table, a place you could vacate if you just picked yourself up and walked off.

Suddenly the pounding took on form and meaning.

Christina rolled her eyes and heaved a sigh of disgust. It wasn't the tide. It was Benj and Mr. Shevvington, and probably that Mr. Gardner. Pounding on the doors, yelling her name. "I forgot I bolted the doors on the inside. Val, you have to hide."

"There's no point in hiding. They know I'm here."

"They think you're in the bedrooms. Go back to the cellar. They'll never look there."

"I can't go back in the cellar. *The alone* will get me."

"There's no such thing as the alone. It won't get you. Take an orange with you." Christina bundled Val toward the cellar door.

"But what about that Mr. Gardner?" cried Val. "What if they take you away and I'm still in the cellar? What if I'm trapped down there forever? Chrissie, you can't do this to me. They're taking you, I can feel them taking you. You —"

"Don't be silly," said Christina, opening the cellar door.

Val staggered down the steps, into the seaweed-slick dark. "No," she whimpered, clinging to the splintery wooden rail with her left hand. With her right hand, she clung to Christina. "You come down here with me," she said, and her fingers wrapped and crawled up Christina to find a better grip.

"I can't. I have to save us. I have to let them in."

"That won't save us! That's how they'll get us. Chrissie, let me back up. Into the light. Into the world. I can't stay down here."

Christina peeled Val off and backed up the steps. "Sssshhh. Don't make any noise."

The cellar made its own noises. Whispering, folding, creaking noises. Noises that slunk forward and crept through their legs. In the dark, among the spiderwebs and the abandoned, moldy boxes of things nobody wanted, Val inched her way to the furnace. It heated water even in the summer. She leaned on it, soaking up its warmth like an infant trying to find a mother substitute.

"You okay?" said Christina. "Can I shut the door now?"

Val laughed insanely.

Christina Romney shut the door.

"She's one of them," Val told the furnace. "She's part of it all. She wants me down here. With *the alone*."

The shadows closed in.

Val's mind shut down.

The furnace chuckled to itself.

Chapter 17

Christina was on the wharf, waiting for her mother to come in on Frankie's boat. It was a clear day: The sea was sparkling glass. Christina felt as if she could see through the curving horizon of ocean all the way to Burning Fog Isle. She loved the wharf: the stacks of lobster traps, the lapping water, the clacking of ropes and chains against flagpoles and masts.

Benj stood as solid as the wooden pilings on which the wharf was built. "Chrissie, what is all this about? Mr. Gardner wouldn't tell me. The Shevvingtons wouldn't tell me. And now you won't tell me, either."

She could not tell him.

The night had been so long. There had been storms, and every streak of lightning and every boom of thunder seemed to call her name. The ocean had raged, hurling itself against the cliff, the waves reaching for Schooner Inne like drowning sailors trying to get out of the water.

She had not slept. She had lain in her warm bed, in her room of fire and islands, and thought of Val, alone in the darkness of the cellar.

At two in the morning she got up. She slid out of bed, slid out of her room, slid toward the stairs — only to find Mr. Shevvington standing there, still in his suit, as if he never undressed, as if he had come that way: tailored and pinstriped and perfect, like a Ken doll you zipped back into its carrying case when you were done playing with him. "Going somewhere, Christina?" said Mr. Shevvington, and he laughed.

"I'm getting a drink of water," she said with dignity.

"The bathroom is the other way," said Mr. Shevvington, smiling, enjoying himself.

Did the Shevvingtons know about *the alone*, creeping up, swarming around their ankles, trying to pull Christina and Val both underwater, to drown in the ocean of their minds? They must. Perhaps *they* were the alone.

She had gotten a drink of water. And stood in the bathroom and wept, because she could not check on Val. Could not tiptoe down and cuddle her in the dark, in the endless night.

I'm wrong, Christina had thought, lying in bed again. I shut her up for no reason. I can't save Val from anything. I'm only making it worse.

She tried to imagine spending an entire night down there in that cellar.

* * *

"Talk to me, Christina!" said Benjamin on the way to the dock to meet Christina's mother the next morning.

She laughed. It was a queer, shaky laugh, because she had had no sleep to back it up. "That's good coming from you," she teased, "who only started talking last week."

Christina stared at Schooner Inne, where she had learned about Evil. The glass in the high cupola caught the morning sun and blinded her. She decided to test Benj. See if he could understand. "Think of Anya," she said to him, picking her words carefully. "The Shevvingtons chose Anya as a victim. They attacked her in every way. Humiliating her, setting her up, terrifying her, undermining her courage. She began to lose her mind. And then her looks, her character, her grades. That's evil, Benj. It's the Shevvingtons' hobby. And with me, with Val, they —"

"Christina, stop it! Anya was trying too hard. She got too nervous to stay in school and she dropped out for a while. It happens to a lot of kids. They take a little rest and they're fine. There is no evil, Chrissie, no plot."

Christina was exhausted and desperate. But Benjamin Jaye was furious. Every bone, every muscle was tight and full of anger. "The reason you've had problems with Mr. and Mrs. Shevvington is your bad attitude, Chrissie. You made up your mind from the beginning not to get along. The very first day in September when we got off Frankie's boat, you were spoiling for a fight. And when spooky things happened, you blamed them on the Shevvingtons. I thought you were making everything up. When we found out about the Shevvingtons' insane son, and that you were right, we apologized, Chrissie. But you still wanted the Shevvingtons to be evil. Evil, evil, evil! That's all we heard from you." Benj took a breath. His lungs filled, his T-shirt stretched, his big shoulders lifted and stayed there. "Christina, some people are dumb and some are mean and some lose their minds, but nobody is evil."

He wants the world to be like himself, thought Christina. Solid and secure and comprehensible. He wants a perfect match: engines that work, tides that change, people who are reliable. Once I thought the world was like that. I thought all parents were like my parents: perfect and loving. I thought all teachers were like my teacher on the Isle: good and kind. I thought all grown-ups could be trusted.

On land and sea, motors roared. Sea gulls screamed and dipped. Benj let out his breath. Like a summer person he stared at the sea and the eternal waves, hoping the rhythm of the world would ease his tension.

Frankie's boat was visible. Her mother would be standing by the rail, hungry to see Christina. Frankie's nasty dog Rindge was barking; his tourist-scaring yap crossed the waves ahead of the boat.

She remembered her grand idea of telephoning all those principals to get the names of girls who had had nervous breakdowns while the Shevvingtons were there. But the personnel secretary — married to that Mr. Gardner — had alerted the Shevvingtons, who doubtless had alerted their allies back in Louisiana and Oregon and Pennsylvania and New Jersey. Christina would never know.

And even if she did get the names, none of those families of the past would blame the Shevvingtons, either.

That was the whole key — make it be the girl's fault. Make her be weak, or stupid, or nervous, or uncooperative.

Never use words like Evil.

People could not accept the presence of Evil. They had to laugh, or shrug. Walk away, or look elsewhere.

Look at Benj, furious with her for not trusting him, and then when she trusted him and told him what was happening, he got even more furious with her for making it up.

My mother will be exactly the same, thought Christina. She wants to talk about buying a dance dress. About summer coming, and her restaurant on the Isle, and how Daddy is repairing the tennis courts, and how summer people are trespassing on the bird nesting preserve again this year. I am alone in the battle.

Unless . . .

Christina was suddenly shot through with hope.

Little crystals of hope tumbled through her mind like fireworks in a distant sky.

. . . unless I can get hold of the briefcase! The one where they keep the Fear Files: the folders with our photographs on them: the only part left of the girls who are in rooms 1 through 6.

I've tried before . . . but I can try again. You can always try again. That's what I am. Granite of the Isle.

The wharf came to life. People waiting for Frankie's boat emerged from cars and off benches. They brought packages to carry to Burning Fog and waved to their friends coming in. The sea gulls screamed for sandwich crusts and the last of the popcorn.

A horn honked in the parking lot on the hill. It beat a tattoo until everybody on the wharf turned to look. "Chrissie!" came a shout. "Hey, Benj! It's me, Anya!" Anya — who had left Schooner Inne so fragile she hardly breathed on her own? Anya — who without Blake would have folded like paper, shut in the envelope of her mind?

Today's Anya danced over the sunburned rocks, tripping down the long, steep wooden steps. Light as a cloud, Anya came to rest against Christina and Benj. "Chrissie," she said, cuddling. "It's wonderful to see you. I've missed you so, living with Blake's aunt in the city. But it gave me time to calm down."

"And be free of the Shevvingtons," said Christina.

Anya's chuckle hit the waves and the waves

tossed it back. "I'm healed, Chrissie. I can hardly wait to be home." She breathed in a great lungful of restorative sea air.

"What healed you?" said Christina.

"Blake's aunt. She made me finish my senior year after all. Did you know you can go to night school, with adults, and still get your credits? And she said the most calming thing is to read how other people stayed calm, so she made me read ancient books of truth: Plato, Isaiah, Marcus Aurelius."

Christina could not imagine choosing a "calming" book. She liked her books packed with action and excitement, preferably murders and chases.

"I need to go to Burning Fog, Chrissie. I need to smell it and see it and walk it!" She was the island princess again, sea spray misting her hair like diamonds. "Here's Frankie's boat! Here's your mother. Oh, Christina, I'm so glad to be going home." She whirled around, shading her eyes against the bright sun, calling upward, "Blake! Hurry!"

Blake was here! Blake, whom Christina had adored with all her strength and mind and soul. Her heart soared, carried by Anya's high, happy voice.

"See, Christina," said Benj. "Nothing evil touched Anya. She just needed a rest. It's true what they say about island girls. There's something about all that isolation. It touches each of you when you get to the mainland. It's harder for you."

He rambled on about Anya and Dolly and Christina. But Christina had forgotten Benj. Forgotten the Shevvingtons. Forgotten evil.

Like a catalog advertisement — windblown hair, fine physique, excellent clothing — Blake leaned against the shining red triangle of his sports car. The car was nothing but an accessory: his was the beauty. When he descended the steps, he was taking over the world. He radiated exciting plans.

Christina yearned to run up to him, fling herself upon him, tell him that he had just lit up the world. But she held herself still. If she touched Blake, she would turn hot and gasping with love. And what would she do with all that love? Blake was not hers. He was Anya's. And even if he were not, she was — rounding off — only fourteen to his eighteen. He would have no use for her puppy love.

"Christina," said Blake, holding out his arms. In his mouth the world was perfection and romance.

"Hi, Blake," she said, not moving. Without permission, her heart took off anyway, thundering down the road to love. In a one-second daydream, Blake forgot Anya, begged Christina to love him, took her to Paris, asked her to marry him.

"No hug?" teased Blake, hugging her anyway. "I've missed you, kid. What a senior year I've endured — Anya off with my aunt in one town, you here at home, and me at that ridiculous boarding school." He grinned. "But I triumphed. Graduated with honors and went back to claim Anya. Knight in shining armor that I am."

Next to this conqueror, how quaint, how dull Benj was.

I am granite, Christina reminded herself.

But she was not. She was Silly Putty.

Frankie's boat docked. Ropes were tossed, mail carried off. Rindge barked like an attack dog. Christina's mother leaped into the huddle of Anya, Blake, Christina, and Benj. Hugging them separately and then all together, she cried, "What a pleasure! How is everybody?"

They all claimed to be "Very well, thank you." They kissed, hugged, said how their parents were, how the weather had been, when graduation was. How well-named was "small talk." This group had no lack of "large" topics: they could talk of Evil, Jealousy, or Nervous Breakdowns, but no, they said how blue the sky was.

"Guess what we're off to do," said Mrs. Romney to Anya and Blake. "Dress shopping." She giggled. "Benj and Christina are going to the sophomore dance together next Friday."

Anya shrieked joyously, the way girls do when romance appears. Blake grinned and shook hands with Benj, who remained solid and silent.

"A landmark occasion," said Mrs. Romney. "My daughter's first dance. I'm so excited."

Benj did not look the least bit excited, but nobody expected him to.

Her mother rattled off department store and dress shop names. "Mother," protested Christina, "some of those are miles away."

"This is an all-day expedition," said Mrs. Romney. "We have to find the perfect dress and you can't do that in a minute."

Frankie leaned on the whistle of his boat. Tourists scrambled on. Groceries, dry cleaning, engine parts, new screen windows were carried aboard. Anya cried, "Good-bye everybody!" She and Blake, holding hands, dashed gracefully onto the boat.

Christina ached to be that hand. To be tightly clasped by Blake.

How could life be so unfair? The only two escaped victims of the Shevvingtons — Anya and Blake — were vanishing again, without admitting the war was still on. What did they think of Christina still living with the Shevvingtons? Did Anya choose not to remember what had really happened to her? Did she, too, think that it had been her own imagination and weakness? Did she think Evil was disposed of forever?

The wind increased. A deep, cruel cloud covered the horizon. The ocean stopped laughing. It slapped the cliffs with its usual anger. On top of Breakneck Hill, Schooner Inne stood alone: its white-clapboard bulk perched on the very edge, ready to tumble off the cliff.

Christina's mother ran up the steep stairs toward the parked cars. She always had energy to spare. "Come on," she cried to Christina and Benj. "Benj, do you want to come shopping with us?"

Benjamin Jaye touched Christina's hair. She could feel her colors. He was touching the gold. He wound her hair around his wrists, binding himself to her by golden ropes. "I'm not going, but get a pretty dress," he said.

She saw that he loved her as a faithful, uncomprehending dog would love her. That he would adore, accept her flaws, and be hers.

For a terrible moment, he seemed nothing but a burden. She wanted to run or fly. To skim away like the terns fluttering so close to the waves. Motionless, Christina stood on the wharf, while her mother and Benjamin Jaye ascended. The bones on her face seemed truly carved of granite. She had been quarried from Burning Fog's deep abandoned pools.

In the cupola of Schooner Inne, sun glinted off a pair of binoculars.

Chapter 18

The afternoon had a cycle.

Mrs. Romney would say, "Darling, that dress looks perfect. I love the neckline."

Christina would say, "Mother, you know what?"

"What, dear? Do you think we want larger flower patterns, like this, like splashy watercolors? Or tiny flower patterns, like this one, sort of Early American?"

How, in the petite section of the dress shop, surrounded by linen and cotton, rayon and blends, was Christina to talk about Evil? She would say, "I'm not sure I want any flowers on the dress at all, Mother. I'm not that much of a flower person." I'm granite, she thought. But none of the dresses looked right for granite.

"Mother," she tried again, "the Shevvingtons are being really awful."

"I know you don't get along, dear, but there are only a few days till school is out. In fact, let's count up so you can start ticking the hours off. Next year they'll be gone, and we'll have better arrangements. I feel terrible that you've had such a difficult year, but you have to remember poor Mr. and Mrs. Shevvington have had a grim year also. Imagine struggling for twenty-five years to bring up your son, and you think at last he's managing on his own — even if it is just a furnished room a few blocks away above a coffee shop — still, you have hope — and what do you learn? He's completely crazy and trying to torment the very young girls you have under your own protection." Mrs. Romney shook her head. "I feel so sorry for them, Chrissie. It breaks my heart. It's every parent's nightmare, that her own child will turn out wrong."

"But Mother, they really are terrible people. I just can't get through to you. The Shevvingtons . . ." but her voice dwindled away. Even to Christina, it no longer seemed possible. This was Maine. The United States. America. Pine woods and crashing seas. Blue skies and loving mother.

Instead of Evil, they talked of Benj, and whether he was romantic and what this dance would lead to. She saw that her mother misunderstood. Her mother thought this was For Eternity. . . . The Future. . . . True Love. All it was was a dance, and Benj was asking the girl he knew best.

"Nonsense," said her mother. "I've seen plenty of boys in love and that one's in love. Now tell me everything. Absolutely everything."

But of course her mother did not mean that at all. Her mother did not want to hear that the Shevvingtons were stuffing her pockets with match books to prove she was a wharf rat. Her mother wanted to hear that Benj had swept her away, kissed her by candlelight.

"Let's go for ice cream," said Christina. "Butterscotch sauce on buttercrunch ice cream, just what you like."

"I love when you remember details," said her mother happily. "We're so close, you and I."

Through the countryside they drove. The road passed between two wide meadows. "Look!" cried her mother, slowing. Three bright blue dots fluttering across the grass. Indigo blue: the color of postcards from the Mediterranean. "Bluebirds," whispered her mother reverently. "I haven't seen a bluebird in years. Chrissie, that's when you know God's in his heaven and all's right with the world. When you see bluebirds again."

Christina could think of several arguments against this. All's *not* right with the world, she thought. I don't know how things will ever be right in Val's world again. I don't even know what world Val will have.

"Mommy, have you heard anything about Val?" she asked.

"Everybody's still searching for her, I guess. She was in Anya's class, I think. A jinxed group if there ever was one. Just one nervous breakdown after another."

"Did you ever think it was — well — planned?"

said Christina. "That somebody made all those things happen on purpose?"

"Don't be silly," said her mother, and quickly drove to another dress shop. Like Benj, her mother wanted only a pretty world, where bluebirds danced in green grass.

The dress they finally found was stark, blinding white. Its shoulders were narrow, laced with tiny ribbons. It had no waist, but fell straight, doubling up at the thighs in pleats and runs of ribbon. "What a twenties' flapper would wear to communion," giggled her mother. "Wild but pure."

If I wore this dress to the storm cottage, thought Christina, you could not tell me apart from the walls and the floors.

"Let's go to the hairdresser," said her mother.

Christina had never had her hair professionally done. It was so tangly, long and thick, there had never seemed any point. Her mother simply trimmed it straight across when it needed it. Their timing was perfect. The mall stylist had an opening just as they walked in.

He washed her hair. The sweet perfume of the conditioner wafted around Christina like mist. He divided her hair into its separate colors, setting them in long, twisting curls. "Banana curls, your grandmother would call those," said her mother. The stylist lifted the gold into a separate section, catching it with a ribbon and letting it fall: a bouquet of golden locks on a silver sea.

When she looked in a mirror she could not see herself. An island nymph sparkled back: a sprite, formed not of earth or flesh, but a swimmer in the sea. Around her, shoppers paused and stared. Other hairdressers, other customers, stood still. She felt all of their eyes, as if they had no bodies: only eyes. Eyes. Eyes.

I am separate, thought Christina, like my hair. I am not one with the world. When I need help, no one will come. No one will recognize me.

Her mother had to rush to catch Frankie's last run back to the Isle. Dropping Christina off in front of Schooner Inne, she barely even stopped the car. "Say hello to the Shevvingtons for me," she cried. Christina's heart answered, *Say hello to Blake for me!* But aloud she called after her mother, "Say hello to Daddy." Her mother drove down Breakneck Hill, honking madly to signal Frankie not to leave without her. Frankie waved his baseball cap in acknowledgment.

Time stopped.

They turned into a photograph: an old, sepia-colored photo in which they would stand forever: Frankie waving a baseball cap, her mother opening a car door. She wanted to scream, *Wait for me!* Wanted to run down there, leap into Eternity with them, and be saved.

But Frankie lowered his cap. Her mother dashed down the wharf steps.

Christina slipped inside the Inne and ran up the

stairs, dress box in hand, and on up to the cupola for the best view of the boat returning to Burning Fog. As she rose up the stairs in the old sea captain's house, a sick feeling rose with her, engulfing her like rising tide. Her mother would never return for her. Or, if her mother returned, Christina would not know. They were parting — minds and souls — forever.

The stairs went on and on. Flight after flight after flight. She seemed to climb into the sky. Into other worlds. Outside the ocean whispered, Ffff-FFFFFFFFFFF. It whispered inside her head, tangling in her hair like seaweed.

FfffFFFFFFFFFFFF, said the house.

FffffFFFFFFFFFFFF, said the sea.

Christina clung to the curly banisters. She was wading in seawater. Tides yanked her under. Her head spun. Her hair blinded her. The house smelled of low tides and rotting fish.

Chhhhhrrrissssssssstinahh, whispered the sea.

Chhhhhrrrissssssssstinahh, whispered the house.

She dropped the dress box. She fell to her knees. The sea sucked her down like mud. Dark, thick, oily mud. "Hello, Christina," whispered the house, in a voice as furry as a leopard's. It wrapped its arms around her. Christina and the sea washed into the empty guest room.

How tired she was from all that shopping. How she yearned to lie down. Perhaps she, like Val, would lie down forever. She would rest and not talk. Sleep and not think.

The bed was soft and welcoming.

Chhhhhrrrisssssssstinahh, whispered the world.

She felt herself turning white and formless, like the furniture in the storm cottage, shapeless beneath the sheets. She was no longer separate from the world, but one with it. Sinking into it by losing her grip on it. She thought of her hair, of its separate colors, but she could no longer feel them. She thought of Blake, but could no longer remember what he looked like. Thought of Benj, but he did not matter.

"Here I am," she said to the house and the sea.

When her eyes closed, she knew she would never open them. She lacked the desire. She would stay deep inside herself, where all was known, all was safe.

She thought of Christina Romney, but even Christina Romney did not seem to matter. She was a person, but the person was not Chrissie Romney, nearly fourteen, end of seventh grade, Maine, USA, the World. She was someone else, floating through time and weather.

Someone ancient and new.

Someone at war and at peace.

"Here I am," she said to the house and the sea.

She lay quietly in the inside of her mind. It was not muddy dark at all, but soft and rocking, like a hammock in the shade.

Outside in the hall, the brass numbers on each guest room door winked and went out like candles.

There was a creaking and a sighing, like the foot-steps of ghosts.

I am a shell, thought Christina.

She did not mind. It was safe and easy, being a shell. No insides to worry about.

"I'll stay," she said to the house and sea.

Chapter 19

"Today's the seventh-grade picnic," said Michael at breakfast.

Mrs. Shevvington had made runny poached eggs. Michael and Benj liked them that way, but Christina did not. But today it didn't matter. Christina had not gotten up. Benj had gone into her bedroom and told her it was time for school. Michael had gone in to say it was time for breakfast. But Christina just lay there.

Mr. Shevvington said, "What a shame. Since Christina won't be in school, she cannot attend the picnic in the evening. For of course the school rule is that you cannot participate in after-school activities if you choose to skip school by day."

"Won't be in school?" said Benj. "Of course she'll be in school. I'll go drag her out of bed."

"She needs her rest," said Mrs. Shevvington. She smiled at her egg and stabbed the little yellow mound with her fork. Yellow yolk spurted over the egg white and ran into the toast. Mrs. Shevvington cut a little square of bread and sopped up the egg yolk with it. It was the kind of thing that made Christina gag. "After the way Christina has been acting," said Mrs. Shevvington, "running away from Mr. Gardner, locking us out of our own house, playing with candles and matches — well! — you know, at the very least, the girl is overtired."

"Overtired?" repeated Mr. Shevvington. His eyebrows reached into his forehead and hid beneath his long, silvery hair. "It's certainly more than that, my dear. We do not wish to frighten her parents unnecessarily. But there is a strong similarity between the mental collapse Anya suffered and what is happening to Christina. Of course, Christina's is so much more serious. So much more dangerous. I have spoken to school and fire department officials and everyone agrees that there is a strong possibility that Christina is the one who — "

"There is not!" shouted Benjamin. He threw his plate across the room. He stared at the plate, broken in two large and several tiny pieces. At the egg on the wall and the flight pattern of yellow across the floor. He had never before in his life thrown anything in a rage.

Mrs. Shevvington smiled at him. "You knew what Mr. Shevvington was going to say, though, didn't you, Benjamin? You cannot deny the thought has passed through your own mind. That Christina's affection for fire borders on the insane. Look at you, making excuses for her, hiding matches from her, snuffing out candles for her."

"She says *you* hid the matches," Benj said.

In the voice of a sad angel, Mrs. Shevvington said, "Benj, Benj. And you believe her? Hers is a true case of paranoia, of believing the world is after her. Here it is the end of the school year. Christina has been studying so hard for exams. It's a struggle for all you island children to keep up with the mainlanders. And poor Christina is desperate to catch up to girls like Gretchen and Vicki. Jealousy eats away at the soul, you know, Benjamin. Poor Christina has the acid of jealousy rusting her heart."

"She's dying to go to the picnic," he said. "And besides, we have a Band Committee meeting today right after school. She has to come."

The Shevvingtons regarded him silently. The silence built, and became a space in the room, something Benjamin could hardly see through, or think past. His mind fumbled to understand what was going on. There were questions to ask; questions to ask Christina; but he did not know what they were, and the thick, hanging silence of the room stilled his tongue.

"And I think it's time you accepted your part of the blame, Benjamin," said Mrs. Shevvington.

"My part of the blame?" repeated Benj. The woman put her arm on his. It felt as sticky as suction cups. He had the creepiest sense that she was attaching herself.

"You demanded that the poor child try to keep up with seniors like Megan and Astrid, Benjamin! Was that not an act of cruelty on your part?"

Benjamin was taken aback.

"And then — you asked her to your sophomore dance. You — age sixteen! Inviting a child, forcing her to try to be sophisticated and adult almost overnight."

"She said yes," Benj defended himself.

"Of course she said yes! You're older and exciting and intriguing. How could she turn you down? Nevertheless, look what all this combined pressure forced her into, Benjamin!"

He was flattered, in a sickening way, to be called exciting and intriguing.

"Coaxing her to do this, pushing her to do that!" Mrs. Shevvington shook her head, appalled. "When you knew — better than any of us — how fragile Christina is! Then purposely adding pressure — *pressure! Pressure!* Demands — *demands! Demands!* On a thirteen-year-old, Benjamin!"

Benjamin mumbled something, ashamed. Michael shifted his weight around on his chair, looking at nobody, as if afraid of infection through eye contact.

"I am shocked, aren't you, that her parents didn't mind?" said Mr. Shevvington. His voice was as cold as glaciers. "Had it been up to us, Benjamin, you may be sure we would have put a stop to your behavior."

"What do you have to say for yourself, Benjamin?" said Mrs. Shevvington softly, forgivingly.

"I guess I used bad judgment," he said helplessly.

"At least you admit it. Although it's too late to

help Christina now. The only decent thing for you to do, Benjamin, is to let the poor child rest. Leave her alone. Completely alone."

Benjamin swirled the orange juice in his glass without drinking it. Michael tore his toast up into little shreds, as if planning to feed ducks.

Mrs. Shevvington said to her husband. "It's a continual surprise to me that a little girl's own parents have so little concern for her emotional well-being."

"At least she'll sleep," said Mr. Shevvington. "Probably the only rest she'll have before the truth comes out."

"What truth?" said Michael nervously.

The house creaked.

Steps above them bent and shuffled.

"She's getting up!" cried Benj, and he ran out of the kitchen, to the bottom of the stairs, looking up. Nobody was there. He ran on up the stairs, taking them two at a time, barreling open the half-closed door to Christina's room. But she was still motionless under the white sheet, as if laid out in a funeral home.

Benj said, "Chrissie, you've got to get up. Pull yourself together!" He wet his lips. He started to say, *I'm here, I love you, I'll stick by you.* But Mrs. Shevvington came into the room, and he could not say words like that in front of witnesses. He was not sure he could say words like that at all.

He meant to give her a hand; haul her bodily out of the bed, prop her on her feet. But how eerily still she lay. He could not bring himself to grab her fingers and pull. She hardly seemed like Christina — more like a shell from which Christina had fled. He caught himself hunching down, peering nervously around, as if Christina's ghost were being prepared in the air above his head, were floating by.

Mrs. Shevvington crossed the room, passed the bed, and reached behind the draperies to find the cord. She pulled them shut slowly, as if closing a lid. The room was dark now, all natural light extinguished. Christina, who gave off light herself, from her golden hair and her shining personality, was dark also. The colors of her hair were meaningless.

Mr. Shevvington emerged silently from behind Benj, as if he had not used his feet to climb, but glided up. "Now, Benjamin. Cheer up. You have a big band meeting today after school for the Disney trip. You've received permission, remember. And you have to put together the fund-raisers."

"Christina was going to work on that," said Benj numbly.

"What a shame," said Mr. Shevvington sadly. "But the senior girls can easily handle it without her."

From the hallway below, Michael yelled, "Come on, Benj, we'll be late."

Benjamin backed onto the balcony. The Shevvingtons came out with him. "Don't worry about her," said Mrs. Shevvington gently. "We all make mistakes. It was a serious one you made with Christina, but as for the fires, you know Benjamin, that was her own choice. So don't feel too bad. And I'll come home at lunch to check on her."

They shut the door to Christina's room.

Down the curling stairs they went, down, and down, and down. Benjamin had the queerest sensation that he was sinking into the bowels of the earth, that he was going down flight after flight after flight. The house whispered and folded around him, its darkness coming up the cracks, crawling upward, seeking light.

He remembered once he had gotten silly on his lobster boat, playing games with Michael, knocking them both overboard. They were both fine swimmers, but it was a long, long way to shore. The boat lazily motored on; the boys swam after it. Swam, and swam, and swam, while the boat teasingly circled out of reach. The boys grew colder, their strokes shorter, their lungs tired. The sea seemed to laugh, tossing waves over their eyes, throwing seaweed over their faces, yanking their feet down.

He felt as if the house were in control of him, as the sea had been once. That he was as close to drowning now as he had been that terrible day.

With relief he reached ground level, followed Michael to the door, stared out into a real world, with real cars and noise and people.

Behind him Mr. and Mrs. Shevvington paused to enfold each other. It was not a hug. It was a wrapping of one around the other. They spread each other's evil and lived on it.

The day was hot. In the parlors and sitting rooms of the old mansion, curtains blew softly in the sea breeze. "The next owners will probably replace all these old drapes," remarked Mrs. Shevvington. "What a shame. They're so historic." She picked up a sheaf of seventh-grade papers, corrected, ready to return, and walked out the door. Mr. Shevvington cradled in his arms the briefcase Christina had so wanted to steal. His fingers lingered on the smooth, supple leather as if stroking a loved one.

The great green doors were shut fast.

Christina was alone.

A shaft of gaudy yellow sunshine, golden as Christina's hair had once been, shot from the cupola glass above to the guest room doors below. Like diamonds, the brass number 8 glittered. Tiny rainbows — shattered pieces of Christina — danced on the balcony walls. Then the sun passed on, the rainbows vanished, and all was quiet.

Christina was gone.

Chapter 20

Seventh-graders splashed down the hallways like waterfalls tumbling. They bubbled and pushed and chattered and laughed. It was an end-of-the-year sound. A we're-almost-free sound. A summer-soon sound.

It ceased at the door to Mrs. Shevvington's English room.

But Mrs. Shevvington amazed them. She was laughing and light herself. She actually joked. She even said they would do no work today, but would be reading a play aloud. She had chosen a play in which there were enough parts to go around for the entire class.

There was one empty seat.

Jonah said, "Where's Christina?"

Mrs. Shevvington said, "She's been feeling a little run-down lately. She decided to sleep in instead of coming to school today."

The class was shocked. They exchanged glances. The picnic wouldn't be any fun without Christina.

Even for Vicki and Gretch it wouldn't be; the whole seventh grade revolved around Christina.

Jonah said slowly, "I can't believe Christina wouldn't be in school today. She knows as well as any of us that if she doesn't attend classes she can't come to the picnic."

"I'm not sure the picnic is quite as important to Christina as it is to you children," said Mrs. Shevvington kindly. "You must remember how homesick these island children become, how desperate she is to get back to Burning Fog."

"But she planned the picnic," said Katy. "She planned the games and she got the grocery store to donate chocolate bars, graham crackers, and marshmallows for the S'mores."

"She got the Sailing Shop to donate prizes," said Gretch suddenly.

"And the Gift Shoppe," said another girl.

Mrs. Shevvington said, "Open your play scripts please. Vicki, I am casting you as Lady Roxbury. In this play, you are a very elegant and beautiful Englishwoman. Can you imitate an English accent, Vicki?"

Jonah said, "I'm going to check on Christina."

Mrs. Shevvington stared at him. Her black pebble eyes glittered. Her thick fingers dripped blood red polish. She took one step toward Jonah. The class flinched. She took another step.

Jonah said, "I want to be sure nothing has happened to Christina."

" 'Happened to Christina'?" repeated Mrs. Shevvington. "What on earth do you mean by that, Jonah?"

Jonah stood up. How scrawny he looked. Mrs. Shevvington was solid as a small refrigerator, or a stacked washer/dryer. Jonah was all dangling bones and uncoordinated joints. "The way things happened to Anya, Mrs. Shevvington."

Her eyebrows flattened.

"The way things happened to Dolly," said Jonah. He was losing his voice; her eyes were freezing him over like ice on a pond. "The way things happened to Val," he whispered.

Mrs. Shevvington's eyes were gone. Her lids closed over them like cracked tan paper shades.

The class shivered.

She opened her eyes and snagged Jonah on them.

"Sit down, Jonah," breathed Katy. "Or things will happen to you."

Mrs. Shevvington's little yellow corn teeth showed. "Katy, Katy. Such imagination. What a shame you are not able to demonstrate it in your homework. Jonah is welcome to check on Christina, of course. But that would be skipping school. He would not be able to attend the picnic either."

"Then Christina and I will have a separate picnic," said Jonah.

Mrs. Shevvington laughed. "Christina is in love with Benjamin, who is sixteen. And also in love with Blake, who is eighteen. Do you think she will even notice a little boy like you attempting to 'save' her?"

Her laugh rattled around like pebbles thrown into a tin bucket.

Jonah flushed.

Vicki and Gretch giggled. "At least you have a brain, Jonah," said Vicki. "Benjamin doesn't. You could offer Chrissie your brain."

"She likes muscles," said Gretch, "and Jonah doesn't have any of those."

"Run along, Jonah," said Mrs. Shevvington. "You may certainly come back to school and report what you find. We'll all be so interested."

Behind Jonah, between the snickering girls, Robbie stood up. He was even scrawnier than Jonah and much shorter, not having started his growth at all. He looked about nine. He said, "I'm going with you Jonah."

Vicki and Gretch burst into gales of laughter. "What a team!" snickered Gretch. "Gosh, I hope when I'm in trouble, I get rescued by men like these."

Mrs. Shevvington's birdseed teeth vanished, as if she had swallowed them herself. "Let's not tease, girls. It's painful to be an adolescent boy with nothing to offer. Let's not make it worse."

The door to the English room creaked.

Slowly, as if the hinges had grown together, it began opening.

The door cried out, rustily, as if it hurt.

The children froze, staring.

Mrs. Shevvington seemed to swell and bloat.

Slowly the door ate its way into the classroom. Gently it tapped the far wall. It shivered against the plaster.

A ray of sun walked across the classroom from the window to the door, like a golden ghost.

Standing in the shaft of light was a tangle of silver and gold: the tri-colored hair of Christina Romney.

She looked at the class. She looked at Robbie and at Jonah, standing up for her. She looked at Vicki and Gretch, laughing at them all. She looked at Mrs. Shevvington. Without a sound . . . slowly, as if wound up . . . she entered the room. She raised her small chin and pointed her small nose forward. "I came to get you, Mrs. Shevvington," said Christina Romney. In her hand she held a sheaf of grayish-white papers: Xeroxed copies. She tapped them against her open palm.

Gretch and Vicki tittered.

Jonah and Robbie sank back into their seats.

Mrs. Shevvington looked like a dead fish on the sand, filled with her own poisons. "You're late, Christina," she whispered, hissing.

"But not too late," said Christina Romney.

"Go to the office. Mr. Shevvington will take care of you."

Christina's soft eyebrows rose like Roman arches, carved on stone. Her chin lifted higher, like a goddess of the sea. "No."

The class gasped. Nobody said "No" to Mrs. Shevvington.

"I beg your pardon?" said Mrs. Shevvington.

"No," repeated Christina softly. "I have to look at you first. You destroyed so many of us, and you nearly destroyed me. I need to look at you first and know that you are just an ordinary person."

"Go to the office!" said Mrs. Shevvington. Her voice was thick.

The sun glittered on Christina's hair. It divided into separate, living creatures, like silver snakes, or sable ribbons. "Val heard you laughing in the night," said Christina. "You shouldn't have laughed. It woke her up."

Mrs. Shevvington's slick tongue wet her mean little lips. She laughed again, but this time it was queer and bubbly, like froth rising on a milk shake.

"Val remembered, long long ago, when you first befriended her, when you first started eating away at her like acid, that you kept a file on her. She remembered that you had copies. And she found them. In the cellar. Damp and moldy, Mrs. Shevvington, but they have the truth in them. The truth about Emily and Wendy, Margaret and Jessica. And all your other victims. Their photographs, your notes, what happened to them, how you did it."

"Who are Jessica and Emily and all?" said Gretch.

"Shells," said Christina.

"My sister?" cried Robbie. "Christina, is Val all right?"

"No," said Christina, "but she's better. She came for me. She woke me. She dressed me. She was the only one who knew how, because she had been there. She had swung in the same hammock."

"Hammock?" said Vicki and Gretch together. "Christina, do you have any idea how weird you sound?"

"Come, Christina," said Mrs. Shevvington. "You and I will go down to the office. You need sedation. Mr. Shevvington and I will help you."

"I will go to the office with you," said Christina. "But I am using the phone there. To end all the terrible things you have been doing."

"Excuse me?" said Mrs. Shevvington, pasting a smile on her oatmeal face.

"No," said Christina, slowly shaking her head back and forth. The silver locks slid over the gold and tangled with the brown. "I will not excuse you. The law will not excuse you. Parents will not excuse you."

"She *has* flipped out," whispered Vicki. "You were right, Mrs. Shevvington. Christina is gone-zo." Vicki and Gretch snickered.

The froth on Mrs. Shevvington's lips spilled over.

"Being crazy is rather pleasant," said Christina, "once they soften it with drugs or sleep. Like a hammock. You just swing quietly in the shade of your mind."

Mrs. Shevvington seemed to rock back and forth, like a swing.

"And Val," said Robbie, "is Val still in the shade?"

"No," said Christina. "She is back."

Mrs. Shevvington licked the froth from her mouth. "Come, my child of the Isle," she said. "We will go read your silly little papers together. And if you call the police, that is fine with me. It's about time they put a stop to your fire-setting and your match-collecting."

They entered the hallway of the middle school together.

Jonah and Robbie tried to follow.

"I think not," said Mrs. Shevvington, closing the door of the seventh-grade English room behind her. She and Christina walked down the long, wide corridors, where no teacher stood, no student passed, no janitor cleaned. Alone, they walked.

"You made a fatal error, Christina," said Mrs. Shevvington. Her smile widened, as if the smile planned to slit her face, as if it were a parasite turning on its own body. "You wanted to gloat. I sympathize. I enjoy gloating." The smile ate like acid into the oatmeal complexion, until Mrs. Shevvington's face vanished and nothing was there but a yellow slit of triumph. *Val is not safe,* said Mrs. Shevvington. Laughing, she whispered, "And neither, my fair island girl, are you."

Chapter 21

They were too far from the seventh-grade class for her to scream for Robbie or Jonah. Too far from the high school halls to scream for Michael or Benjamin Jaye. They were in the front lobby, by the school offices, where only parents and teachers went willingly.

Mrs. Shevvington stumped on. It was like the evening they went for ice cream, and she struggled in Michael's grip like a kitten dragged to the vet.

Jonah knew this would happen, thought Christina. He told me I was getting cocky. But I had to show off. I had to sashay in there, so the seventh grade would know. I was playing games. But this isn't a game. Don't I know that best? But even so, I kept playing games, thinking I would win.

The grown-ups always win.

In lock-step Mrs. Shevvington and Christina entered the outer office. Filing cabinet drawers were half open while secretaries pretended to look things up. A gym coach without a class lounged on the counter and a big kid getting suspended slouched against the wall.

The staff glanced up. "Oh! Mrs. Shevvington!" they said, ignoring Christina. "Mr. Shevvington just left! Poor little Val showed up after all this time!"

Christina cried out.

"Mr. Shevvington was so sweet to her," put in the file clerk, not answering her ringing phone. "Val was so strange. You would not have believed the accusations she made. The poor child. A clinical case of paranoia if I ever saw one. Just like on soap operas. And she comes from such a nice family, too."

"She was supposed to stay at the Inne," mumbled Christina. "Where she'd be safe."

The gym coach slapped the counter with his huge flat hand. "You're the one who was hiding Val?" he demanded. "You're one of those island girls, aren't you? The one who plays with matches and tried to set a storm cottage on fire. I heard about you. Kids like you shouldn't be allowed in the school system with regular kids."

Christina ripped loose from Mrs. Shevvington and tried to bolt. The gym coach caught Christina's elbows and pinned her to the wall. "This has been some year!" he said to Mrs. Shevvington. "I bet you guys are sorry you ever transferred to Maine. We've handed you more crazies than the rest of the country has in a generation!"

Mrs. Shevvington smiled. There was a puffiness to her now: a contentment. "So true," said Mrs.

Shevvington. "You might call the ambulance for Christina. She must be sedated."

Christina remembered the quiet of the guest room, the painted isles, and the foggy mind. I'll be back there in a minute, she thought. Or in the Institute. And I won't know, or care. I'll be a shell again. What made Val come here? What made either of us come here? Did the Shevvingtons pull us in with their evil or did something in us want to be defeated?

Christina felt herself fading like a sheet in the storm cottage, drifting into mists of mindlessness. Perhaps you had to participate in your own ending. You had to allow it to happen.

"Mr. Shevvington was going to call Val's parents from Schooner Inne," said the file clerk, "for privacy. He always puts the child first, you know. No matter how undeserving. He drove Val back there."

"Did my husband have his briefcase?" asked Mrs. Shevvington.

"Why, yes," said the typist, "I believe he went back into the office to get it. He had Val in one hand and the briefcase in the other."

The coach released Christina's arms. Defeat was so complete that she went limp and sagged to the floor. He knelt beside her. "I'd better get her a glass of water."

The typist said, "I'll call the nurse."

"No need," said Mrs. Shevvington, retrieving the pile of papers that had slipped out of Christina's hands.

"She might be ill," protested the coach. "Sometimes when my students act weird out on the field, it turns out to be heatstroke or something."

"The ambulance is coming. Some things are better left to trained paramedics."

Christina was not ill. She was faking. She leaped to her feet, shoving Mrs. Shevvington against the door. She raced out of the office, skidding on waxy floors toward the front doors. "Stop her!" cried Mrs. Shevvington. "She's dangerous."

Gym coach, secretary, and teacher lurched after Christina.

The big kid getting suspended yawned, stretched, and stuck his feet out. "Oh, sorry," he said pleasantly, when they tripped over him and knocked into each other, bottling up their own exit.

Through the lobby, out the doors, down the wide granite steps, Christina tried to soak granite through her shoes; she would need it all. She heard them coming after her, but the women were wearing narrow skirts and high heels; the coach made kids exercise but rarely exercised himself; Christina was too fleet of foot for them.

Across the wide green expanse of campus she ran. The coach tried to catch her, but Mrs. Shevvington didn't bother. She headed for her car. Christina swerved through the trees, cutting through the opening in the fence. Mrs. Shevvington started her engine. Christina burst out onto the sidewalk, ran down School Street, heading for town. Mrs. Shevvington, driving in the most ordinary way, without unseemly haste, could go forty miles an hour. The woman turned onto the School Street and accelerated.

Christina, sobbing for breath, ran up a side street, crossed two backyards, ducked down a driveway, and came out behind the laundromat. Through the laundromat, between the clattering washers and the steamy dryers, she went. Anya had worked here. Mindlessly folding other people's underwear. Don't let them catch me! prayed Christina.

She crossed Seaside Avenue, and jumped up onto the sidewalk just as Mrs. Shevvington drove across Seaside. She's not trying to catch me, thought Christina. She's going straight to Schooner Inne.

Christina came out at the bottom of Breakneck Hill. Mrs. Shevvington came out at the top and parked in front of Schooner Inne. She unlocked the huge green door, let herself in, and shut it behind her.

I have to get Val, thought Christina. I did this. This is my fault. How did it happen?

Christina stepped over the cliff. She had come up these rocks, but never gone down. Tide was out. The mudflats were slimy and pockmarked. She climbed carefully down the treacherous crags and outcroppings. She had to drop down into the mud. It sucked her in almost to the knees. She tugged her right foot free, and it came out black with slime. Slogging across the flats, mud sucking at her feet, Christina stayed next to the cliffs. No windows in

Schooner Inne could see a person at the bottom of the cliff. In some places the mud had dried and she walked on top. In some places there was water a foot deep, or even two feet, and she waded, or fell in.

She made her way around a jutting stone with sharp edges, and there, hidden in a cleft, was the entrance to the cellar passage the old sea captain had used for smuggling. They would not be expecting her to arrive this way. They would look for her by road, by door, but not by cellar. Tearing her hands, ripping her clothes, she finally got up to the opening. The opening she and Dolly had found so tantalizing—had fallen out of, and nearly been swallowed by the tide while the Shevvingtons' insane son laughed joyfully above.

Christina tiptoed up the splintery wooden cellar steps. How many horrible sounds had she heard in this black hole? How many times had she been cornered here? But today it was her secret entry. Creeping up from the cellar — as the Shevvingtons' son had done in his time — she would slip unnoticed into the house, as Mr. and Mrs. Shevvington watched for her from the doors and windows, and silently she and Val would go back to the sea. Just as she had done with Dolly! They would sail back to the Isle and be safe. Somehow Christina would make all the parents believe her.

Her heart was thudding painfully. Her feet slid muddily inside her own shoes. Pressing her ear against the door that opened into the kitchen, she listened for the silence that would mean she could ease herself inside the house.

"Christina's here," said Mr. Shevvington, laughing. "Open the door, Valerie dear, and let her in."

The kitchen door opened and Christina fell onto the linoleum. Val, whimpering, crowded up against her.

Mr. Shevvington laughed and laughed. The laughter whipped him back and forth, like a flag in the wind. "Come," he said gaily. "Follow me."

The girls followed as if on leashes.

"What's happening?" said Christina. She was crying. All her pain, all her dangerous effort — and for what?

"We thought you'd enjoy watching your so-called proof burn up," said Mrs. Shevvington. "We have files on you, Christina, dear, and on Val of course. On Anya and Dolly. But there are other names. Emily. Margaret. Jessica. Wendy. And oh, so many more! And it will continue, of course. We will never stop."

The wind from the sea came up the cellar passage and tossed the kitchen door back and forth, in a wet, ghostly, low-tide way.

"But we have learned a little something from you, Christina," said Mr. Shevvington. "I just want you to know that first. You taught us not to write anything down and not to save it. So when you're in your little cot, swallowing your little pills, watching your little television, you remember how generous you were to us. Helping us out."

"And giving us," said Mrs. Shevvington, beaming, "such an exciting year. Christina, you were a worthy opponent. I have truly enjoyed bringing you down."

Christina halted at the door to the parlor. "Come on, Val," she said, trying not to let her voice shake, "let's just go out the front door."

"You cannot get out the front door, my dear," said Mrs. Shevvington. "Or any other door. There are bolts, as you well know. There is no exit from this house, Christina, darling. And the windows, too, are locked. The only way out is through the cellar. And what good would that do you? Because the tide is rising."

The tide whiffled and puffed between the cliffs. The sound of the sea blowing out its birthday candles. Candle Cove.

"You and Dolly managed it once, my dear. Late last winter. And you survived. But I doubt if you would be so lucky again." Mrs. Shevvington laughed. "Would you like to light the fire, Christina, dear? Since you so enjoy playing with matches? Would you like to see yourself go up in smoke?"

Val shivered up against Christina like a draft. "It's my fault," she said, weeping on Christina. "I thought I was doing the right thing. I wanted the whole town to see how terrible they are, so I thought I would start with the school and the teachers and tell them out loud what the Shevvingtons have been doing. But they thought I was crazy."

We *were* crazy, thought Christina, to believe for

a single moment that we could beat Authority. People are dogs on leashes. They follow the biggest and the strongest, not the small and weak. "It's all right," said Christina, patting Val. To the Shevvingtons she said, "What are you going to do with us after you burn all those papers?"

Mr. Shevvington laughed. "Christina, you know better," he chided gently. "We won't do anything to you. Your own families, your own neighbors, perhaps your own boyfriend, will do things to you. Get you psychiatrists, medications, institutional care. This is America, the end of the twentieth century. We don't take care of our mentally deranged at home. We hospitalize them. Otherwise they would upset us." His voice was like old velvet: soft, but cracked.

The girls were pushed into the parlor.

Mr. Shevvington picked one file out of his bulging briefcase. From his jacket pocket he took a slim, gold-trimmed fountain pen. In neat black ink he added a brief notation. Then he handed the file to Christina.

It was her own. Dated the first day of school, the past September. On that day they had chosen her, had opened her file. And the new writing was today's date.

This day in May, before she was fourteen, before she went to the dance, before she had her first date, before she danced in her innocent white dress — Christina Romney's file would close.

Mr. and Mrs. Shevvington lit a real fire in the fireplace with the sea-green mantel. The mantel arched over the cold stone. The fire caught. While Christina clung to her own file, Mr. Shevvington drew another from his beloved briefcase. "Jessica," he said lovingly to his wife.

"Jessica," she nodded, and they smiled, remembering. They crumpled all the evidence of Jessica — perhaps all that Jessica was or ever would be now — and tossed it onto the fire, smiling, smiling, smiling. The fire flickered and smiled back, like an ally. Like an old friend.

The day was hot. Mrs. Shevvington crossed the parlor with its dark flocked walls and pushed aside the thick ancient curtains, with their linings as ancient and rotten as her own mind. She thrust open the window.

The curtains swayed in the breeze.

The scent of roses, wisteria vines, and sea grass reached their noses; the perfumes of Christina's world. Of her own space on this earth. Of Burning Fog Isle.

Come to me! thought Christina. Come save me. I am Christina of the Isle, and I need you.

Sea wind raced over the waves, lifting them into great curls, like fingers of the dead.

Sea wind separated the three colors of her hair: again, she was silver and gold and sable.

Sea wind coursed through the dry, old house. It

came in through the cellar passage, and passed through the kitchen, and crept into the hallways, invisibly swirling and twisting.

It entered every room, looking for a way out.

Jessica burst into flames.

Mrs. Shevvington added Emily.

The wind kicked the parlor door open.

The door slammed against the wall, as if an angry ghost had stormed in.

The Shevvingtons turned, alarmed. But nothing was there. "For a minute, I thought Christina had found a way out," laughed Mr. Shevvington. He tossed crunched-up remains of Emily into the fire.

Nothing visible had been added to the room.

But the wind had come: Christina's wind, of the Isle.

Chapter 22

Sea wind reached into the shallow fireplace. It lifted the crumpled, flaming balls of paper that were Jessica and Emily. There was no grate, no screen. The wind hurled the smouldering proof across the room into the dry, silken, old drapes.

The curtains caught fire in the blink of an eye. They turned silver and gold and then immediately were nothing but black char, falling to the floor.

The green-flocked wallpaper caught fire.

The intricate, creamy wooden molding around the windows caught fire.

The old spindled tables and elegant varnished chairs caught fire.

Val screamed. Christina and Val backed into the hall. Mr. and Mrs. Shevvington came right after them. Mr. Shevvington said calmly to his wife, "Just shut the door, my dear. Stopping the draft will stop the fire."

Christina grabbed Val's hand and they ran up

the stairs. Up, up, and up, to the only place left to go, to the cupola.

But the parlor door was as old as the curtains, and it no longer met at the edges. Flames licked through the cracks like long yellow tongues. The fire ran ahead of the wind, snatching curtains and furniture, old walls and ancient beams.

The parlor was consumed.

The fire reached for the hall.

More! cried the house, which the Shevvingtons had wired to whisper names and evil thoughts.

More! cried the wind, which the Shevvingtons had caused to whistle through tiny holes and frighten fragile Anya.

More! cried the sea, whose tides the Shevvingtons had used to swallow Dolly.

Christina coughed.

Val choked.

Down below, Mr. Shevvington said, "Just unlock the front door my dear, and we'll go next door and be safe. What a pity the girls forgot elementary safety rules. Anybody knows that fire and smoke rise."

Val was fastening herself so tightly to Christina that it was like wearing another layer of extremely heavy clothing. Christina reached the final step. With scrabbling fingers she struggled to find the latches that would release the cupola windows. They opened outward to a narrow wooden ledge where once there had been a widow's walk. Christina had been out there once. But the latches were too tight for her to budge. Or else they, too, were locked. Christina's small fingers were the right size to get under the little latches, but too small to have enough force to open them.

"The fire will burn the floor out from under our feet," sobbed Val.

Below them, Mr. Shevvington said, "Open the bolt, my dear."

"I'm trying," said Mrs. Shevvington. "I can't see it. There's too much smoke."

Christina could not see her latches either in the dark swirls. "Hold your breath, Val," she muttered. Her lungs seared with pain, from the hot smoke or from needing another fresh breath. But she did not breathe. She fought with the latch. "I can't get it," she said to Val.

"We're going to burn to death," whispered Val.

Downstairs, Mrs. Shevvington screamed, "I got the bolt out. But where are the keys? We have to get the lock, too! Give me your keys!"

"No, we're not," said Christina. She kicked in the window. Glass spattered out into the air and shot through the sky. Glass, and only glass, leaped over the roof and fell below on the rocks of Candle Cove. High tide thundered in to meet it. The spray of waves met the spray of falling glass and no eye could tell one from the other.

Christina stepped out onto the ledge, dragging Val with her. "It's over for me now," said Christina dully. "I might as well step off into Candle Cove."

"What do you mean?" cried Val sucking in wonderful clean ocean air, laughing in the blue sky. "We got out! You did it, Christina! We're going to be all right. Look, somebody's already reported the fire. I hear sirens. We're so high up I bet we can see the firehouse doors open. Yes — here comes the first truck! They'll take us down the ladder."

Great heat rose up the stairwell, as if in a huge, stepped chimney. Wreaths of smoke danced around the two girls. Under their feet they could feel the temperature increasing. Val danced lightly on the narrow wooden shelf.

In the road fire engines gleamed scarlet, with the brightness that only fire engines have. Two kinds of sirens screamed. Tourists yanked cars halfway onto sidewalks and children turned to see where the fire engines were going.

Christina and Val could see the whole village, the whole school complex. Christina thought of the seventh grade, and what they would think of her. Of Jonah and Benjamin, of Anya and Blake, but most of all, of her mother and father.

"The Shevvingtons will tell everybody I lit the fire," said Christina. "The Shevvingtons will say I did this. They'll have all their terrible stories to back it up. Nobody will believe me. Not ever."

The first shining truck came out of the narrow roads above Breakneck Hill Road. Breakneck Hill was named for a little boy who a hundred years before had ridden a bike down it, and lost control. I'm in control now, thought Christina. But I never will be again. The Shevvingtons have won.

A ladder wound off the top of the immense truck, like some enormous chain necklace. On the pavement, firemen began yanking on huge protective yellow and black suits. Val screamed and yelled and waved as if it were a Halloween parade.

"You go first," said Christina, as the fireman began coming up the ladder toward them.

She stood alone on the ledge, her hair blowing in the wind from Burning Fog Isle. Under her feet, the ancient wood crackled and burned. For Christina, the worst nightmare had come true. She was alone, friendless, and lost. Forever, and ever, and ever.

Chapter 23

It was a very tiny airplane.

From where Christina stood, between Mr. Gardner and Mrs. Gardner, it looked like a paper airplane a seventh-grader might throw across the room when the teacher wasn't looking.

"I thought my parents would come in on Frankie's boat," she said.

"Certainly not," said Mr. Gardner. "Not when it's this much of an emergency. They chartered a plane." He picked Christina up, as if she were three or four years old, instead of nearly fourteen. He hugged her hard and said, "They love you, Christina. They'll be here in a minute."

"You see, Christina," said the fire chief, standing behind Mr. Gardner, "the only fingerprints we found at the storm cottage were Mrs. Shevvington's. That made us wonder. Why had she trespassed? It's one thing for a little girl like you to slip into a locked summer house — but the seventh-grade teacher? And then both Robbie and Jonah came to us, telling us that they were pretty sure that Mrs. Shevvington was stuffing your purse and pockets with matches. That was such a sick and frightening image. I couldn't get it out of my mind."

"And," said Mrs. Gardner, the personnel secretary, "I made those telephone calls, Christina. I adored the Shevvingtons. I admit it. I thought they were wonderful. Loving, caring, generous. But I reached people in Oregon, in Louisiana, and in Pennsylvania, with stories like Val's. Like Anya's. Like yours. You were absolutely right, Christina. It was their hobby. The way some couples collect antiques or refinish cars, the Shevvingtons like to destroy."

"And when they were trying to label you a wharf rat," said Mr. Gardner, "even saying your mother and father were — why, we've known your family forever, Christina. It was impossible. Why would they say things like that? What was the point? I kept turning it over in my mind."

"We were slow figuring it out," said Mrs. Gardner. She rubbed Christina's back, comforting her. "We didn't want to admit that we had brought into our community a man and a woman who were genuine sadists. People who would start rumors for the joy of seeing the damage." She suddenly clung to Christina's shoulder, as if even Mrs. Gardner needed to hang onto the granite that was Christina Romney. "We began to see," said Mrs. Gardner, "that of course if you like to hurt people, you would choose a child who can't fight back. And in this town, you would choose an island child, whose parents are not there to see. And you would choose the sweet ones, because where would the pleasure be in hurting the nasty kids? The fun is the emptying of a soul everybody loves, not a soul everybody loathes."

The fun, thought Christina.

Their final moment had not been fun.

"I feel terrible that you had to go through so much torture, Christina," said Mr. Gardner, "before we did our part in stopping the Shevvingtons. All the same, I wish it hadn't ended like that."

Everybody turned involuntarily, to look back across the cove and the village at the cliff where once a huge white sea captain's house had stood. Schooner Inne was gone. No sooner had Val and Christina been scooped off the cupola than flames shot from every window and the entire building turned black and collapsed. Nobody could have gotten out.

"We got a video," said another fireman. "What a shot! You girls will want to see that."

Christina did not think so. She remembered the screams from beneath her feet, when flames took the carpet under Mrs. Shevvington's heels, when the woman ran from room to room screaming, "Where are my keys?" When flames melted the doorknob under Mr. Shevvington's hand, and he jerked back, screaming, "Get the keys!"

The fireman said to Christina, "You'll be fantastic on that film footage. The way you stood on that ledge, your hair blowing in the wind, looking for all the world like the figurehead of some ancient sailing ship, pointing toward justice and port."

The tiny plane landed, bounced, slowed down, and taxied toward them. Christina freed herself from the Gardners and ran toward her mother and father. The little door opened and out popped her mother, holding out her arms, crying her daughter's name. And then her father, shouting, "Christina!" The plane motor cut the syllables of her name up into sections, and vibrated them across the pavement.

And then she was safe, wrapped in her family.

They held the seventh-grade picnic anyway. The school board said it would frighten the children to have to think about what Mr. and Mrs. Shevvington were really like, and it was best to have them think about three-legged races and watermelon seed-spitting contests instead. "We don't want our little boys and girls to have any knowledge of evil," said the man who had hired the Shevvingtons.

Christina thought that was silly. The more knowledge you had of evil, the better you could combat it. How could anybody learn from what she had been through if nobody would admit it had happened? Out there somewhere, in another state, in another village, another thirteen-year-old girl might come face to face with evil for the first time. She had to know what to do, how to tell the world.

The smell of wet towels and bathing suits filled the air. They had a lip-sync contest and a Frisbee toss. They had corn on the cob and blueberry cobbler. Parents stood around laughing, teachers sat cross-legged swatting gnats, and neighbors looked yearningly at the games, wishing they were children again.

Christina's parents could not stop hugging her, holding her, telling her how wonderful she was. "You triumphed," said her father. "You won."

"And without us," said her mother sadly. "We didn't believe you. I will never forgive myself that we didn't believe you."

Mr. and Mrs. Armstrong were awkward with Val. Christina could imagine why. How would it feel to know you had put the opinion of the high school principal ahead of the word of your daughter? How would it feel to know that your child had spent a year under lock, key, and tranquilizers because you did not believe in her?

Close, thought Christina. I came so close.

Blake came, and Anya, and they, too, hugged her and said how proud they were of her courage. Christina was surprised to find that a hug from Blake was only a hug; it did not take away her senses and fling her into crazy love. It was just two arms.

And when they walked away, she thought, I was the one with courage. Not Blake. He could have come back weekends from his boarding school. He could have spoken up for me after the thing with the cliff. But he was afraid he would sound dumb, and people would think he made it all up. So he said nothing.

She took a marshmallow when her father offered her one, and poked a green twig through it.

There were many marshmallow-roasting techniques. Some people liked to get their marshmallow an even, light tan all over, and some liked to set it on fire, and some liked it to start dripping down the stick so you could lick it up, tongue-burning hot and crispy black on the outside.

Like Schooner Inne.

They had brought forth what they said was Mr. and Mrs. Shevvington. It was teeth, actually, and belt buckles, and bones.

When Anya had been afraid of the poster of the sea, she had thought she could see the hands of the drowned reaching up through the waves. The sea wants one of us! she had cried.

The sea had two now. By its wind and tide, it had set its own fires to take the Shevvingtons.

I was afraid, she thought. More afraid than Blake or Benj could ever know. And nobody believed me. But I was born in the arms of Good, and I am made of granite, and if I had let them go — Anya and Dolly and Val — I would have been Evil myself.

There is Evil in silence.

But there is no silence at a seventh-grade picnic.

Rock music jarred Christina awake. Throbbing, strumming guitars, drums, and electric keyboards.

The seventh grade was dancing without her. Everybody was dancing. Summer people and townspeople, firemen and teachers, parents and children.

The music screamed; the tide slapped; the sun set.

Her father and mother danced; Mr. and Mrs. Gardner danced; Mr. and Mrs. Armstrong danced. Blake danced with Anya and then he danced with Val.

It's primitive, thought Christina. Like ancient warriors by the sea, we are having our funeral celebration for the death of Evil among us.

Benjamin and Jonah came toward her, one from the sea and one from the land. One with broad shoulders and strong arms, one with long skinny legs and a long skinny smile.

The boys hardly saw each other. They had eyes only for Christina of the Isle. And, at the same time, they said, "Chrissie? Let's dance." Each held out a hand. The silver and gold of Christina's strange hair divided, and tangled, and told her secrets.

She remembered all that was to come: the sophomore dance, the fund-raising for the band trip to Disney World, the ferry on which Jonah could come, the lobster boat she could go out on with Benjamin. Summer on Burning Fog. The roses that bloomed among the rocks and the cats that had kittens in the barns.

"Oh, yes," said Christina Romney. "There is so much to dance for."

And she took both hands.

About the Author

CAROLINE COONEY lives in a small seacoast village in Connecticut, with three children and two pianos. She writes every day on a word processor and then goes for a long walk down the beach to figure out what she's going to write the following day. She's written about thirty-five books for young people, but *The Fog*, *The Snow*, and *The Fire* is her first horror series. She also plays the piano for the school music programs, is learning jazz, reads a mystery novel a night, and does a lot of embroidery.

point®

Other books you will enjoy,
about real kids like you!

THRILLERS

Gripping tales that will keep you turning from page to page - strange
happenings, unsolved mysteries, and things unimaginable!